The Boy N

Two Stories :

My Dream Boy

I think I've always known I was different from most of my buddies. It seemed that from the time we all got puberty they were a lot more interested in girls and pussy than I was. I can remember in freshman gym class when some of us started getting pubic hair and when our dicks began to get bigger, I was always turned on when I saw their floppy cocks and low hanging balls. Oh of course I played along with them about liking girls and dated several girls in high school but my heart wasn't in it.

Near the end of my freshman year of college my eyes were opened. I was nineteen constantly horny and after classes one day a couple of my friends and I were sitting in the student union talking.

"I'm so fucking horny," my pal Joey said. "If I don't find some girl to fuck tonight I'm going to have to take a drive down to Corrida Park."

"That's a sure thing," my other friend Todd said.

I was in the dark.

"What the hell are you talking about?"

"You never heard of Corrida Park?"

"Of course, it's a little park on the south side of town, so what?"

"It's a gay cruising place. Gay men hang out there and they'll give you a blow job no problem."

"All you have to do is go there and in no time one will be slurping on your boner," Todd said.

"No shit? How come I never heard of it before? I said.

"You must lead a sheltered life Jake. I thought everyone knew about it."

"Have either of you done it?" I asked.

Todd turned red.

"You have?"

"I got drunk just before Christmas break and went down there."

"And?"

"I parked the car and got out. It wasn't real cold so I walked down a trail that went into the woods. I was only a little way down the trail and this guy walked up and said hi. He asked me what I was looking for. I said I needed a blow job."

"Holy shit, just like that?"

"Well he had his eyes right on my crotch, so I knew he was interested."

"Then what?"

"He led me into a little opening in the trees and knelt down in front of me. He unbuckled my belt, unfastened my pants and pulled them and my boxers down. My cock was hard as a rock. He stroked it a little and licked some precum off the tip and then took the damn thing down his throat. It only took me three minutes and I came in his mouth."

I felt my cock getting hard.

"Oh man," I said.

"He sucked you off just like that?" Joey asked.

"Yeah, he loved it," Todd answered.

"I heard that you could get sucked off there but I never had the guts to try it," Joey said.

"Damn," I said.

"So how was it?" Joey asked.

"Fucking great. The guy knew how to suck a cock. He did a lot better job than my girlfriend does."

Joey looked at me and shook his head. "Damn."

Todd looked at the clock.

"Shit I'm gonna be late for class," he said. He jumped up and sprinted across the union to the door.

"That's something," I said.

"No shit. I heard of it but didn't know he'd gone there," Joey said.

We sat there for a few minutes quietly. I think both of us were thinking the same thing.

"Would you ever do that?" I asked.

"It'd be scary. But it does sound hot. I haven't had a blow job since New Year's Eve."

Fuck, I'd never had a blowjob but didn't tell Joey that.

"How about you?" he asked.

"I don't know. I think it'd be scary too. It would be better if you went with someone."

"Hey, that's a good idea."

"What? You mean you want to go there?"

"Why not? It's just blow and go. They don't expect anything in return."

My dick was hard as a hammer handle.

"Fuck, I've got such a boner," I said grinning.

"Me too."

He sat there and grinned at me.

"Let's do it."

"Now?"

"Are you done with classes for the day?"

"Well yeah, I guess I am."

"So am I."

I looked at Joey and grinned. He was a cute guy. He has an adorable face and really nice black hair and deep brown eyes. He's a medium sized guy with a great body and is as cute as they come. The idea of seeing him getting a blowjob turned me on.

"I'll drive," I said.

"Fucking A!"

We both stood up and I could plainly see Joey's boner in his shorts. He was wearing plaid shorts and a red tee shirt with sandals on his feet.

"I can see your cock," I said.

He looked at mine.

"I can see yours too. Better put your books in front."

We both hid our boners behind our books and walked to the dorm parking lot. We jumped in my car.

I looked over and could see Joey's hard-on. It looked pretty big. He looked at mine too.

"Kind of horny huh?" he said grinning.

"Yeah, I've got a boner that won't quit."

We drove to the little park. There were cars parked in the parking lot and a few men sitting on benches.

"What do we do now?" I asked.

"I don't know. I suppose we get out and take a walk."

"Let's stay together," I said.

"Yeah, I'm pretty nervous. I'd feel safer if both of us are together," he said.

I was wearing cargo shorts and a tank top. I'm nearly six feet tall and pretty fit. While I'm not what you'd call drop-dead handsome, I think I'm pretty good looking. My hair is longish and light brown. In the summer it gets to what they call dirty blond.

Joey and I walked along the edge of the park and saw a trail that led off into the woods. Joey looked and me and I shrugged and we walked down the trail.

"I wonder if somebody will approach us?" I whispered.

"I don't know. Fuck I'm nervous," he said.

"We can just go back," I said.

"No I gotta cum, I'm too fucking horny now."

We didn't go far and two guys stepped out of a little side trail. They were both in their late 30's or 40's. One was short and kind of skinny and the other was taller and a little heavy. They were both rubbing their cocks.

"Hey, how are you two hotties?" one of them said.

"We're horny," Joey said.

I nodded.

"Well you came to the right place," the heavyset guy said.

"Step into our office," the short one said.

We followed them down the side trail and it went to a little opening in the trees. They stopped and turned and stepped up to us. The short one was in front of Joey and the taller one was in front of me.

"Would it be okay if we feel your cocks?" the short one asked.

I nodded and Joey said, "Yeah, go ahead."

"You two are over 18," he said.

"We're both 19," Joey replied.

The tall guy took hold of my cock through my pants and began rubbing up and down the shaft.

"Oh yeah, that's a nice one," he said.

I looked and the other one had his hand on Joey's cock and Joey had his eyes closed.

"You better get that thing out or I'm gonna cum in my pants," Joey said.

The guy dropped to his knees and undid Joey's shorts and pulled them to the ground. His cock popped up and it looked really nice. It looked to be about six inches long and pretty thick. It had an upward curve and a nice head on it. His balls hung down loose and his pubes were thick and black.

The guy in front of me looked at me and I nodded yes. He dropped to his knees and pulled my shorts and boxers down and gasped.

"Oh my you have a beauty," he said.

My cock is also about six inches but thicker than most I've ever seen. My balls are pretty large and I keep my light brown pubes trimmed a little. I don't like shaved pubes but do like them neat.

The guy opened his mouth and took my cock all the way down his throat. I couldn't believe he could do that. His nose was brushing my pubes. I could feel his throat constricting on my cock and it felt amazing.

Joey let out a gasp and I saw the guy sucking him swallowing. Joey's knees began shaking as he came in the guy's mouth.

The guy in front of me slid back so just my dick head was in his lips and then took me deeply again. He grabbed my balls and played with them and then sucked my dick head again and I began cumming. I thought I was going to pass out. He slurped on my cock and didn't miss a drop of cum.

The two guys looked at each other and grinned. I looked over at Joey and he was also grinning.

"Fucking A," he said.

"Did you enjoy it?" the short guy asked.

"Damn right. Sorry about cumming so quick. I was pretty horny," Joey said.

"Me too," I said, "That was my first time with a guy sucking me and I got pretty excited."

"You guys come back any time," the tall one said

"There are other things we can do for you that will make you feel real good too," the short one said.

Joey and I pulled up our pants and tucked our semi-hard cocks in them.

"Thank you," I said.

Joey did the same.

We walked out of the little clearing a little unsteady. We got to the car and Joey looked over at me. "That was damn nice," he said.

"A hell of a lot better than jacking off," I said.

We both had grins on our faces as we drove back to campus.

"You fuckers! Why didn't you wait for me," Todd said when we told him we'd gotten blowjobs at the park."

"You had class," I said.

"You couldn't wait one hour?"

"We had boners," Joey said grinning.

"Well fuck," Todd said. "Who wants to go back with me?"

"I've got a late chemistry lab," Joey said.

"How about it Jake?" he said to me.

"I just got a blow job two hours ago."

"So what? Are you telling me you can't get another boner now?"

Well that was true. I could get a boner ten minutes after I jacked off. And that blowjob did really feel good. Plus I'd be able to see Todd's cock hard.

"Okay, let's go," I said.

Todd beamed. Joey was pissed.

"I'll be fucking around with chemicals and you two will be getting head. Fuck me."

We took my car and drove to the park. Todd was stroking his cock through his pants. I tried not to look too obvious but it was pretty hot watching him play with his cock and balls. Todd is a cute guy who looks like he's three years younger than he is. Actually he's almost 20 but looks much younger. He wrestled in high school and is on the wrestling team at college so he's not only boyish looking but small too. He wrestles at 126 pounds and is a compact little dynamo with blond hair and blue eyes and muscles that won't quit. I've watched him many times on the mat in his wrestling uniform that is not much more than a tank top and a pair of boxer briefs. His cock and balls are right there in the open and I've boned up watching him many times. Now I was going to get to see it naked and hard.

"I hope there's some guys there yet," he said.

"Why do you think they'll all be gone?"

"It's nearly dinner time. They might all have gone home."

"Well then you'll have to blow me," I said.

"Yeah right," he said grinning.

There weren't any cars in the parking lot.

"Fuck it looks like nobody's here," I said.

"Let's get out and see."

We got out and walked down the trail to the woods. Each time there was a side -trail we checked it out. Many had condom wrappers and used condoms lying on the grass.

"Damn litterbugs," Todd said.

We were about to give up when we saw someone in the bushes.

"Hey," Todd said.

A young guy came out of the trees. He wasn't much older than we were, maybe in his mid-twenties.

"Hi," he said shyly.

He looked pretty nervous. He was thin and wearing gym shorts and a tee shirt. He had on flip-flops and it was easy to see his cock in his shorts.

"What's up?" Todd said.

"Oh just relaxing," the kid said.

"Not many guys around now," I said.

"Yeah the old guys go home this late."

There was an awkward pause.

"So do you…?"

He nodded. "I wouldn't mind," he said.

Todd motioned for him to follow us and we walked down a side trail. There was a blanket lying on the ground.

"That's mine," the kid said. "I was sunning."

"Cool," Todd said. "I could use a little sun too."

Todd looked at me and something clicked. I knew what he had in mind… and I liked it."

Todd began taking his clothes off and so did the kid and I. In a minute we were all naked. I'd seen Todd's cock soft at the wrestling matches and now I could see it hard. It stood up right against his belly and the head was right at his belly button. It was a hell of a nice cock for a small guy. His balls were large and hung down real low. His pubes were short and trimmed into a triangle shape.

The kid had a nice cock maybe five inches or a bit more, low balls and he was shaved. He had a nice body and was pretty cute.

"What's your name?" I asked as I reached over and held his cock.

He shuddered when I touched him.

"I'm Alex," he whispered.

Todd was stroking his cock. He looked at me and put his hand on my cock and began stroking it. Holy shit, this was getting pretty damn hot.

The kid took Todd's cock and began jacking him.

"Let's lie down," Todd said.

We lay down and it was obvious what was going to happen. Each of our heads was at the cock of one of the other guys. I looked at Todd and he looked me in the eye and nodded.

I nodded back and Todd took my cock in his mouth. Holy shit.

I leaned down and took the kid's cock in my mouth. I'd thought of doing this for a long time and it was just as fantastic as I dreamed it would be. His cock smelled like clean boy and tasted lovely. The kid started sucking Todd.

As excited as I was I knew it wouldn't be long before I came. Todd didn't suck me as well as the older guy did but he was doing his best. I took the kid's cock from my mouth and licked his balls making him moan.

Todd began making a whimpering sound and the kid swallowed and went to his pubes as Todd came in his mouth. Todd ran his tongue around my cock head and that set me off. I felt my balls crunch up and I shot cum into my buddy's mouth. Todd swallowed every drop of it.

The kid was lying back enjoying his cock in my mouth. Todd surprised me when he got up and knelt by the kid's face… and kissed him on the mouth!

The kid moaned and I felt hot cum shooting into my mouth. I'd tasted my own before so it wasn't a surprise. He shot a lot of cum and I swallowed it and then let his cock slip from my mouth.

We all lay there basking in the sun and panting.

"Fuck, that was hot," I said.

"It didn't freak you out?" Todd asked.

"Uh uh."

The kid sat up. "Wow thanks for that. I didn't expect to get my dick sucked today. I hoped to suck one and then jack off."

"It was nice to meet you Alex," I said.

"Likewise" he said grinning.

"Well, I'm hungry now," Todd said.

We all dressed and walked back to the parking lot. Alex said he lived just a couple of blocks away. We thanked him for a good time and got in the car.

It was a little awkward for a bit.

"So you're okay with what happened?" Todd asked.

"Yeah, actually I really liked it," I said.

"That wasn't my first time," Todd said.

"You mean sucking a guy?"

He nodded. "I've done it a few times," he said.

"Wow, so you're bi?"

"I guess," he said.

"Nothing wrong with that," I said.

"Who did you do it to before?" I asked.

"One of the wrestlers," he said.

"Do you want to name names?"

He grinned. "He'd break me in half if I did. You understand. You wouldn't want me to tell anyone what we did."

"Yeah I get it. Was it that guy with the curly brown hair who wrestled at 165?"

"Not telling," he said grinning.

"So maybe we can do it again sometime?"

I grinned at him.

"Definitely."

"I'm starved," I said as we pulled into campus. "Let's go get dinner."

We walked to the cafeteria and went through the line. We'd just sat down when Joey came up.

"Well?" he asked with a grin on his face.

We both smiled.

"You fuckers! Damn now I'm going to have to go back to the dorm and jack off."

"Sorry," I said.

"Well eat slow, I'm going to get my food. I want to hear all about it."

Joey hurried off.

"What are we gonna tell him?" Todd asked.

"I dunno, maybe just tell him a couple of guys sucked us off?"

"I suppose. I wonder what he'd think about what we really did?"

"You mean tell him?" I lowered my voice, "that we sucked cock?"

He shrugged. "He's pretty open-minded."

"Wow what happens if he freaks?"

"Well I don't think he'll freak. At least I hope not he's a good buddy and I'd hate to lose him as a friend. We are pretty open about stuff and I think he's not uptight about guys doing shit to each other."

"Well we better decide, here he comes," I said.

Joey sat down. "Ok was it the same two guys?" he asked excitedly.

"No there was only one guy there when we got there. It was getting kind of late I guess," I said.

"So he did you both?"

I looked at Todd.

"Not exactly," he said.

"What do you mean not exactly? Did he suck you off or not?"

"Well he sucked me off while we were doing a three-way."

Joey sat there a second. "A three way?"

"He sucked me while I sucked Jake and while Jake sucked this kid who we met there."

I held my breath. Joey sat there looking confused and then I could see the light come on.

"You guys sucked cock too?"

We both nodded.

"No fucking way!"

"It just happened," I said.

"You guys sucked cock?"

"Jeez Joey, quiet down, the whole room will hear you."

"Oops, sorry. So let me get this straight. Todd you sucked Jake and he sucked this random guy and that guy sucked you."

"Correct. The guy was about our age. He had a blanket on the ground back in one of those little cubby holes and we laid head to cock, so to speak and sucked each other off," I said.

Joey sat looking dumbfounded.

"Well fuck me."

Todd and I didn't know for sure what to say.

"So does this mean you're gay?" Joey asked.

"I've done it before," Todd said. "I like girls too. So I guess I'm bi."

"I've had sex with girls but I think I prefer guys," I said.

"Well as I said before… fuck me."

He sat there and picked up a French fry and shoved it into his mouth.

"So… when are we gonna try this?"

He had a huge grin on his face and Todd and I broke out laughing.

"You want to try it?" I asked.

"I've been curious about that for a long time. I've always wondered what it would be like to have a dick in my mouth. I tried to suck my own but it's not long enough. I never had the balls to try it with someone though. But I'd like to with two good friends like you guys."

"Eat up!" Todd said.

Todd and Joey roomed together so we went to their room. It was a typical messy dorm room with two twin beds.

"How the hell are we gonna do this?" Joey asked.

"Let's push the beds back against the wall and put the mattresses on the floor," I suggested.

They liked that idea and in no time we had our little sex nest ready. We all kind of looked at each other and then we began stripping. In less than a minute we were all naked.

"Oh yeah, this is gonna be fun," Joey said jumping up and down with his boner bouncing.

"Fuck Jake your cock is fat," he said.

"Try it," I said turning toward him.

He grinned and knelt on the mattress on the floor. I stepped over to him and he grabbed my cock. He looked at it up close.

"Damn thing could put an eye out," he said jacking it a bit.

"Suck it," I said.

He opened his mouth and about half of my cock disappeared into it. I moaned as his tongue swirled around my cock head.

"Do me, do me," Todd said.

I pulled away from Joey long enough for the three of us to lay down head to cock. Joey went right back after my cock and I took Todd's in my mouth. I had to pull it away from his belly to get at it. Todd went right down on Joey's cock and Joey yelped when he put it in his mouth.

"Watch the teeth," he said.

"Sorry," Todd said with a mouthful of cock.

We went to work on each other's cocks and everything was pretty quiet except for an occasional slurping sound.

"Suck my balls," Todd said.

He lifted up his leg and I took one of his balls in my mouth. I sucked on it and then sucked the other. While I was there I looked and could see his little pink puckered asshole. It looked pretty cool, so I ran my fingertip across it.

"Oh fuck," Todd said.

"Like that?" I asked.

"Wow that was wicked. Do it some more."

"What?" Joey asked.

"He's fingering my butt hole," Todd said.

"Do me, do me," Joey said.

Soon he began moaning so I figured Todd was fingering his hole. Then I felt Joey licking my balls and soon he was licking farther down.

"Joey what the hell are you doing?" I asked.

"I'm pleasuring you," he said.

"No shit, that feels great," I said.

I could feel his finger rubbing my asshole. Damn it felt good. Then my hole felt wet.

"What are you putting in there?" I asked.

"My tongue," he said.

"You're licking his butt?" Todd said.

"Fucking A."

The next thing we knew we all were licking the other's assholes. And it felt amazing.

We sucked and licked and it took nearly half an hour for us all to get to that point of no return. Todd came first and then I shot and then Joey let a blast shoot into Todd's mouth.

We all lay there sweating and breathing hard. Finally one by one we all sat up on the mattress. I looked at my two friends both sitting there flushed with the afterglow of fresh sex.

"Well?" I said.

"Why is it that we took so long to do this?" Joey said. "All the times we've jacked off we could have been sucking each other off."

We all laughed and decided to take a shower. They lent me a towel and we wrapped them around our waists and walked to the shower room. There were a couple of other guys in there and they looked a little at our red cocks but didn't say anything. After we'd showered we went back and fixed their room back up and I got dressed and left for my own room.

I studied for a couple of hours and then got in bed in my boxers. I closed my eyes and thought of the dicks and balls I'd played with that day and my mind was made up. I damn sure liked that better than when I'd dated girls. The problem was that we only had a few weeks of school left so my newfound suck buddies and I would be parting company in a short time. Damn.

The next day I saw the guys and after the excitement of the new sexual things we'd done I could sense a little regret from Todd. He seemed a little distant and I decided to let it go and see how it played out.

I ran into Joey and asked him about it at lunch.

"Oh he's got his panties in a bunch. He thinks he's going to turn into a flaming queen," he said.

"That's not good," I said.

"Oh don't worry about him. He'll get over it. Shit the more I thought about it the more I liked the idea. I'm not done with girls but this gives me twice the chance at some cum making. I see nothing wrong with that."

I grinned at my horny buddy. As cute as he was he'd get all the pussy and cock he wanted.

I saw Todd later and asked him how he was doing.

"I'm okay," he said.

"Are you having second thoughts?"

"About yesterday?"

I nodded.

"I've been thinking about it," he said.

"Todd it's not that big a deal. I've read that nearly all guys either have a gay experience or want to sometime in their lives. I wouldn't worry about it."

"So you don't think I'll buy a pair of high heels and start singing a song from Hello Dolly?"

I laughed. "I doubt it."

"Well, yeah I guess you're right," he said. "That stuff we did made me cum harder than I've cum in a long time. I guess that's a good thing."

The school year wound down and we had just a couple of days left before we were going to leave for home. The three of us went out for pizza and talked a kid who worked at the pizza joint into selling us a pitcher of beer. Todd had a fake ID so he went along with it even though he knew we were underage. We ended up drinking three pitchers of beer and were feeling no pain when we got back to the dorm. My roommate had finished early and was already gone home.

"Well, what are you guy gonna do now?" I asked.

"I dunno, I'm not sleepy," Joey said.

"Any ideas," he asked looking at me.

"Um I was just thinking we won't see each other all summer. I thought maybe we could... um fool around a little."

Joey smiled. "Fucking A."

Todd looked at us.

"You want to?"

I nodded. Joey nodded.

"Only if you want to Todd. I know you've had second thoughts."

"Well it's been a while since we did it and I haven't hidden in a toilet and sucked any cocks so I think I can control myself," he said.

"So is that a yes?" I asked.

"Let's get naked," he said.

It was the end of the day and I wanted us to be nice and fresh because I wanted to do some ass-play with them.

"Let's take a shower first so we're all nice and sweet."

They grinned. "Let's go," Todd said.

We all stripped and wrapped a towel around our waist and ran to the shower. It was empty and we got in and turned on three spigots and began washing. Soon we were washing each other and that turned into washing each other's cocks and balls and assholes. We all had boners and were giggling and laughing like a bunch of teenage girls. I purposely dropped my soap and Joey bent over to pick it up. I stepped up behind him and stuck my hard-on into his butt crack.

"Oy!" he yelled.

I grabbed his hips and rubbed my cock up and down his crack.

"Oh fuck, that feels naughty," he said.

Todd watched us and was mesmerized by our fooling around.

"We should go back," he said quietly.

Joey and I stopped messing around and we dried off and ran back to the room naked. Todd locked the door and we stood there naked with hard cocks.

"That looked pretty exciting," Todd said.

"You mean my cock in his butt?"

He nodded.

"Have you ever put something in your butt?" he asked.

"I've stuck my finger in it," I said.

"I put my brothers toy rocket in my ass," Joey said.

What?

Todd and I turned to Joey.

"You put what in your ass?"

Joey grinned.

"My little brother got a Cape Canaveral space set for Christmas a few years ago. I was on my way to the shower and there sat a rocket. I picked it up and for some reason I took it with me to the shower."

I looked at Todd and we grinned.

"So I'm all soapy and I began to run my finger up and down my ass crack and I picked up the rocket and put it in there. It felt really good, so I began jacking off. When I came I shot cum clear up on the shower door. I don't think I ever came that hard."

"No shit. I've heard that but never heard anyone who actually did it," Todd said.

"Well that was the little rocket," Joey began.

Todd and I began laughing.

"So the next time I took the big one, the Saturn Five, and I put that in there."

"And?"

"I fucking near passed out."

We were all slowly jacking ourselves as he told the story. Todd had a big drop of precum hanging from his cock. The head on mine was all wet and Joey's was leaking like a faucet.

"Let's try it," Todd said.

"Fucking?"

He nodded.

"Oh man that's a big step," Joey said.

"Are you sure Todd?" I asked.

"Hey we've come this far. Let's try it."

"You got any condoms?"

Joey grinned and opened his desk drawer. He had a twelve pack.

"Who's going to do who?"

"Todd it was your idea."

"Jake I want you to fuck me," he said.

"My cock's pretty fat, are you sure?"

"Let's do it before I chicken out."

Joey ripped open a condom pack. He put the condom on my dick head and rolled it down my cock. Then he lubed it up with a tube of lube.

He was jacking me and I got the feeling.

"Stop that or I'll cum before I get it in," I said grabbing his hand.

He grinned. "Damn I like that fat fucker," he said.

"How should we do it?" I Said to Todd.

"Let's try it doggie style."

Joey's cock was dripping and he got down on his bed so he could watch. Todd knelt on the bed and I got behind him. I pulled his ass cheeks apart and ran my finger up his crack. His asshole clinched when I went across it.

"Oh fuck that feels wicked."

I held my fingers out and Joey put some lube on them. Then I stuck one and then another in Todd's ass. He moaned and groaned.

"Ready?"

"Go slow," he said.

I put my dick head at his hole. Fuck there was no way that thing was going in that little hole. I pushed and Todd groaned but suddenly his asshole opened up and my dick head slipped in. His ass muscle grabbed it.

"Oh fuck," I said when I felt my dick begin to throb. "Hold still or I'm gonna cum right now."

I closed my eyes and concentrated and soon the tickling went away. I pushed in a little farther.

"Are you okay?" I asked.

"Yeah, this is great," Joey said.

"Not you asshole. I mean Todd."

"I'm good. Man it feels like I've got a fucking ball bat in there. At first it hurt and I almost said to take it out but now it's feeling pretty good."

I pushed a little farther and slowly worked it until my whole cock was in his ass.

"That's it," I said.

"Fucking amazing," Joey said. His face was just a few inches from my cock and Todd's asshole.

"Can you see well enough?" I asked.

"Yeah, move it in and out a little hey?"

I began fucking Todd's ass. Damn it was tight and it felt hot and amazing.

Joey reached around and grabbed Todd's cock.

"Oh Joe be careful I'm gonna cum if you do that," Todd said.

"You can cum again," Joey said. He jacked Todd a couple of times and his cock exploded with cum shooting out all over the bedspread. It didn't just squirt like normal, it shot out like it was from a faucet. I felt his ass ring clenching at my cock and I began to shoot into the condom.

"Oh my God, I think I my balls exploded," he panted. "I can feel you cumming in side me."

He collapsed on the bed and I went down with him. My cock was still in his ass and it began shriveling up. Soon it slipped from his ass and I got to my feet.

Joey pulled on my cock.

"I think it'd dead," he said.

"Give it mouth to mouth," I said.

He grinned and pulled the condom off and then he put my cock in his mouth and licked off all the cum.

"Horny shit," I said.

Joey grinned up at me. He took hold of his boner and shook it.

"Who wants a treat?"

"Todd?" I asked.

"I gotta rest for a minute. Damn you were right Joey, having something in your ass makes you cum ten times as hard. Why don't you two do it?"

Joey grinned at me.

"On your knees... bitch!"

I slapped him in the balls lightly and knelt on the clean bed. Joey rolled a condom down his cock and lubed it up. Then he lubed my ass. He stuck two fingers in me and it felt damn good. I could hardly wait for his cock to take their place.

"Ready?" he asked.

"Go ahead, but don't just bone me. Take your time."

"Yes sir," he said.

It hurt pretty badly when he pushed his dickhead against my asshole.

"Relax," he said.

I tried to relax my hole and suddenly the head slid in. Wow that hurt.

"Oh fuck, wait a minute," I gasped.

"I won't move," Joey said.

By now Todd was up and sitting on the edge of the other bed watching.

"It'll quit hurting in a minute," he said.

He was right, my ass started to feel better and I felt like I wanted more in it.

"Okay but go slow," I said.

Joey worked his cock into me. I felt his balls slapping against mine.

"Is it all in?"

"Right to the hilt," he said.

"Feels tight but it does feel good," I said.

"See I told you," Todd said.

Joey began fucking my ass. The more he did it the better it felt.

Todd had a boner now and was stroking it. I reached down with one hand and stroked my own cock.

"Let me," Todd said.

I expected him to reach under me and jack me off but he lay on the bed on his back and took my cock in his mouth.

"Oh fuck," I said.

It didn't take long. Joey increased his speed and Todd took my cock deep into his throat. Joey slammed into me and I felt his cock throbbing. Todd went deep on my cock and I began shooting cum into his mouth. My ears started ringing and I thought I was going to faint.

I collapsed on the bed and Todd was still under me. He shimmied out from under my cock and grinned.

"Did that feel good?" he asked.

"Oh fuck, if I'd been wearing shoes that would have blown them off," I panted.

Joey held up a quarter full condom.

"Look at all that cum," he said proudly.

"You're such a stud," Todd said.

We all lay back and rested. I wasn't sure if we were going to do more or not. Finally Todd sat up.

"Well I'm the only one who hasn't fucked someone. It was my idea so I guess it's my turn."

"I'm up," Joey said smiling at his roommate.

"How do you want to do it? Like we did?"

"I want to be on my back. What do they call it, the missionary position? Who the hell thought that one up?"

"Lay down…pastor."

Joey lay on the bed and raised his legs up over his head. His cute little hole winked up at us. He clenched his asshole and it looked like a little blinking eye.

Todd knelt on the end of the bed and bent down and licked Joey's hole.

"Oh man!" Joey said.

I opened a condom and helped Todd roll it down his cock. I knew he could do it but I liked handling his cock anyway. We lubed him up and he put it up to Joey's hole.

"Ready?"

"Let'r rip," Joey said.

Todd worked his cock into Joey. The little fart took it like a man. When Todd was all the way in Joey wrapped his legs around Todd. They ended up belly to belly on the bed fucking like they'd done all their lives.

"Oh yeah, that feels amazing," Joey said.

I sat and watched and suddenly I was pretty surprised. Joey and Todd began kissing. At first Todd just leaned down and pecked Joey on the cheek. Then they kissed on the lips and in no time they were making out like lovers.

My cock was as hard as a pool cue. Damn it was hot watching them. They weren't just fucking…they were making love.

After several minutes Joey began to moan and he tightened up. Todd pushed deeply into him and I could tell he was cumming. They lay there for a minute and then they kissed passionately. Todd looked up and me and blushed.

He got up and his semi-soft cock slipped from Joey's ass. I was surprised when I saw Joey's belly. It was covered with cum.

"You came without touching it?"

"Fuck that was the hottest thing I've ever done, way better than a Saturn Five rocket."

We all laughed like mad. My two best friends and I had all just had gay sex and for some reason we all felt it was just fine. Damn.

We cleaned up and sat naked on the bed.

"Jake, that kissing, I don't know how that happened," Todd said.

"Todd it was beautiful. I was surprised but watching you two making love and kissing was absolutely beautiful. If you'd been with a cute girl it wouldn't have been any more beautiful. It was cool," I said.

"So you're not freaked?"

"Fuck no. Actually I'm a little jealous."

Todd leaned over and kissed me. Wow, he was a good kisser.

"There, now you don't have to feel left out."

It was bittersweet a few days later when we all packed up our stuff and headed for home. Todd and Joey both lived in Madison so they were together. They had plans on getting jobs together if they could find them. We promised that we'd keep in touch during the summer.

"Next year we don't have to live in the dorm," Joey said.

"Maybe we can find a place and share an apartment."

"Fuck yeah, that would be amazing," I said thinking of the fun we could have.

"Well we'll text if we figure something out."

Todd stepped up and we hugged.

"I'll miss you Jake," he said into my ear. "I'm glad we did that stuff together."

"I'll miss you too Todd. These last few weeks have been great."

Joey and I hugged. He grabbed my ass.

"I plan on tapping that ass of yours when we come back," he said.

"Is that a promise?"

"Damn right."

He gave me a kiss on the lips.

They drove off.

My heart felt empty. Damn I loved these guys and I'd miss the shit out of them for the next few months.

I got in my car and headed home feeling kind of lonely.

My parents were happy to have me home and it *was* good to be back but after the fun and freedom of a year in college it was kind of a let down to move back into my room. Everything seemed so…juvenile.

I settled in and it quickly became apparent that I needed something to keep me busy and something I could do to make some money. I got a copy of the daily paper and began looking for jobs. There wasn't much.

I drove downtown and applied at several places and then decided to stop at Taco Bell for lunch. I went in and ordered and while I was waiting I noticed a sign for Help Wanted.

"Is there someone I can talk to about a job?" I asked the counter girl.

"Let me get the manager," she said.

Soon a young guy came out. He was the assistant manager's assistant and his name was Guy. I think he was a high school kid. He said they were looking for a couple of counter workers and cooks. I got an application and filled it out.

He looked it over.

"Well the assistant manager just resigned and we're getting a new one but for now I'm in charge," he said.

"So can you hire?"

"I guess so. Do you want to start tomorrow?"

I grinned. "Damn right," I said.

I filled out all the paperwork and he got me some uniforms and told me to be back then next day at 9-am. Then he gave me my tacos for free. Damn if that wasn't a lucky break to stop there.

My parents both worked and left at 7-am returning at 6-pm. I got some hamburger from the freezer and had things ready to cook on the grill when they got home. They were happy about that and while we ate I told them of my new job.

"So our college boy is now a taco-bender," my dad said.

"Si," I replied.

As we ate I noticed the house next door looked kind of shabby.

"What's with Mrs. Beran? Her house looks like crap."

"Oh she died Honey," my mom said.

"We heard someone bought it. I'm not sure but the rumor is that they're moving in soon," Dad said. "I heard they were coming from California. I hope they're not hippies."

"Well they need to cut the grass," I said.

"All in good time I expect," Dad said.

I reported for work the next day and it was a pretty good job. Guy taught me all the things that needed to be done and the others treated me like a friend. My eight hours went by pretty fast.

When I got home I saw a moving van parked next door. My new neighbors were moving in.

The houses on our block are all the same. A developer started on one end of the block and worked right down the line building one house after another with the same set of plans. When they were all finished the only thing that set them apart was the color of the siding and roof shingles. My room was on the second floor on the side next to the new neighbors.

I stripped and took a shower and put on a pair of boxers and a tank top. I turned on my TV and watched a ball game for a while just chilling.

I heard someone talking and looked out of the window. There was a middle-aged couple talking in the driveway. The man was short and dark. He looked like he was a Mexican or from some other South American country. The woman was a head taller and a blond bombshell. They made a quite a strange couple.

"Hmm, he must have a huge dick to get a good looking woman like that," I thought to myself.

I started to sit back down and heard another voice. I looked again and there was a young guy coming out of the moving van carrying a chair. Wow! He was a hottie.

"Evan, put that in the guest bedroom," his mom said.

I watched the kid. Well he probably wasn't a kid. He looked a little older than me but he was young and damn cute. He was as tall as his mom and had very nice features like she did but he had his dad's coloring and dark hair and eyes. His hair was short and preppy looking. He was wearing cotton shorts and a sleeveless tee shirt. His arms looked really fit and I could see little patches of dark armpit hair. He was wearing sandals.

I felt my cock stir. Damn maybe this summer might not be so lonely after all. He probably wasn't gay but at least I'd have someone to hang out with.

I stood to the side of the window for the next hour or so and watched him carrying stuff into the house. Finally he had all of the small stuff inside and all that was left was the big furniture.

"Mom, how are we going to get that stuff in? Dad can't lift after his surgery. Can you call someone?" he asked.

"Who do we call Honey? We don't know anyone here."

"Well what are we going to do?"

I threw on my sneakers and ran downstairs. When I got to the door I slowed down and sort of ambled out onto the front driveway. I looked over and he was looking my way.

I waved. "Hi," I said.

He smiled a wide smile and his teeth were sparkling white against his darker skin.

"I couldn't help but hear you need a helping hand."

"Oh man that'd be great," he said.

His mom beamed. "Oh how nice," she said.

I walked over and stuck out my hand.

"I'm Jake," I said.

He took my hand. Oh man. His hand was soft yet strong. He shook with a good grip but not a bone-crushing grip like some guys do to make them look like studs.

"Evan," he said.

I followed him in the van. There were about a dozen chairs, dressers and tables in there and we took them one by one and carried them to the appropriate rooms. By the time we got done we were both sweating. His mom got us a couple of sodas and we sat on the patio in back of the house.

"Man thanks, I'd have never gotten all of that stuff in by myself," he said.

"No problem if we're going to be neighbors we it's only right that we help each other out."

I looked him over trying not to be too obvious. Up close he was even cuter than I'd thought. His eyes were so dark brown that they were nearly black. His skin was like an end of summer tan and smooth and lovely. He had a thick patch of black hair under each arm and a little hair on the lower part of his legs. His feet were beautiful. I don't know what it is but I've always had a little fetish for guy's feet.

"How old are you Jake?" he asked.

"I'm 18 but I'll be 19 in about five weeks," I said.

"In school?"

"Yeah, I just finished my first year."

"I'm 22," he said. "I've got one more year of school. I'm going to transfer to a school nearer here. I've been at the U. of Southern California. That's too far to go now."

His mom brought out a bag of tortilla chips and a dish of salsa. She thanked me again for helping.

I took some chips and dipped and ate them. Evan reached across to the table to get some chips and I looked down. I almost shit.

His dick head was peeking out of the leg of his shorts. When he reached it must have slipped out. He took some chips and sat back. I could see just the tip of it yet.

He must have felt a draft because he rearranged his dick and it was gone, but what I saw looked really nice. I felt my cock thickening.

Oh fuck!

"Shit I just remembered I've got to go downtown and pick something up for my mom," I said.

I stood up and started across the yard to our house.

"Hey Jake, I owe you one," Evan said.

"No problem. It was good to meet you."

I got in the house and was fully boned up. Shit. What to do? I told him I had to run downtown and here I had a big boner. I wanted to jack off but he'd wonder why I was in such a big hurry if I didn't leave the house.

"Boy next time come up with a better story," I said to myself.

I got in my car and backed out of the driveway. Evan was putting the moving blankets in the moving van and waved to me.

Damn, I was going to be jacking off a lot this summer.

I drove to a little corner grocery and bought a loaf of bread. Then I drove back like that was what I had forgotten. The moving van was gone and so was the car that had been in the driveway.

I went up to my room and took off my clothes and got in the shower. The warm water was running over me and I closed my eyes and pictured Evan. I could see the tip of his cock sticking out of his shorts. It looked lovely. I knew for sure he was circumcised and that his cock head was pink. I guess that wasn't much but it was a start. Of course I had a hard on and so I began jacking off.

I remembered how Joey's cock had felt in my ass when I came and I stuck my finger up my ass. It wasn't as satisfying as Joey's cock but it made my cock get even harder than it had been. I closed my eyes and came all over the shower door. Man that finger in my ass was a hell of a thing. I was shuddering as I finally stopped oozing cum from my cock.

I finished my shower and got out and dried off. I carried my towel into my bedroom and walked over to my dresser to get a pair of clean boxers. I opened the drawer and grabbed a pair and lifted my leg to put them on when I happened to look in the mirror on the dresser. Evan was across the space between our two houses in his bedroom… and he was watching me.

I quickly decided not to let him know I knew he was watching. I kept my back to him and scratched my ass. Then I bent over and let him get a good look at my hole. When I looked in the mirror again he was gone. Damn.

I heard my parents downstairs so I pulled on a pair of shorts and a tee shirt and went down for dinner.

"Did you meet the new neighbors?" my mom asked.

"Yeah, I met the mother and the son."

"Are they nice?"

"They seem nice. The dad has a bad back or something so I didn't talk to him but I did talk to the mother. The dad is Mexican and the mom looks like a Norwegian or Dane. The son is about my age."

"How nice, maybe you can become friends."

Jeez Mom I'm not six anymore.

"Yeah he seems nice. His name is Evan."

"What are the other's names?"

"I have no idea," I said.

Actually I didn't give a shit. The only one I was interested in was Evan.

The next day I got up and got ready for work. I snuck a look across the way to Evan's room. His curtains were shut. Damn. I went to work and the time went fast because we were busy all day. I'd taken a pair of shorts and a tee with me to work and changed before I left so I wouldn't have to wear the messy uniform home. When I got home Evan was pushing a little mower around the yard trying to cut the foot tall grass.

"Need a hand?" I asked as I got out of my car.

"I need a tractor with a hay maker on it."

"It did get a little out of hand. We've got a rider. Let me get it and I'll ride and you can trim."

"No shit? That'd be great," he said.

"Be back in a minute."

I went in the house and up to my room. I put on a pair of gym shorts and left my boxers on the bed. Then I ran downstairs and got the mower from the garage. I drove it across the driveway and started mowing swaths across their yard. Even went behind me and trimmed around the sidewalk and bushes.

We finished the front and I drove around to the back. When I started across is I pulled the leg of my shorts up a little and let the head of my cock stick out. I'd see if Evan looked and if he did...how long he'd look.

We mowed the grass and after a while I rode past Evan. He grinned as I went past and then I saw him look at my dick. He looked and then looked away. Then he looked again. Bingo.

When we finished his mom came out and thanked me profusely. She insisted we have some sodas and cookies so we sat on the patio.

"Man that was great," Evan said. "I'd have been at this all evening."

"Hey it's no problem. We're neighbors, that's what neighbors do."

I saw him glance at my crotch again. My dick had slid back in when I sat down. I reached for a cookie and it slipped out again. This time about an inch and a half was showing.

Evan seemed a little nervous. "So what do you do in this town for excitement?" he asked.

"The usual, movies, ballgames, fishing."

"You fish?"

"Yeah, I like to fish, do you?"

"I've only done it a few times," he said.

He took a good look at my cock.

"So maybe one of these days we can go fishing," I said.

"Huh?"

"I said maybe you and I can go fishing."

'Oh sure, that'd be fun. I'm not very good at it. You'd have to teach me."

"I'm a good teacher," I said.

I felt my cock beginning to grow. Oh shit!

"Well I better get home. I've got some stuff to do," I said hurrying.

"Thanks Jake, I owe you two favors now," he said.

We bumped fists and I noticed he looked down and it was pretty obvious I was partially boned up.

I got on the mower and drove it home. I ran upstairs and stripped off my clothes and headed to the shower. I stopped at my desk and opened the drawer. I had a yellow highlighter in it and I grabbed it and took it to the shower.

I lathered up my balls and dick and then lathered my asshole. Then I took the highlighter and put it in my ass. Oh yeah, that was even better than a finger. I closed my eyes and pictured Evan...naked. My balls hurt when I came, it was that intense.

Since I was low man on the totem pole at Taco Bell I got the job of mopping out the toilets. Someone had pissed all over the place in the men's and I was in there with a mop and a bucket cleaning it up.

"Here he is," I heard Guy, the assistant manager's assistant say.

"Jake, this is the new assistant manager."

I turned around and there stood Guy... and Evan.

"Evan? You're working here?"

"You guys know each other?" Guy asked.

"We live next door to each other," Evan said.

"Well kiss my ass," Guy said. "That's a coincidence."

"Well I guess you're my boss now," I said.

"Yeah right. This is cool. This is my first day on the job and I already have a best friend."

Wow, I'm his best friend? Holy shit.

Everyone loved Evan. He was cool as the boss and of course the girls went wet in the crotch over his looks. Even some of the guys seemed infatuated with him. Of course who was I to criticize? I was in love with him.

We both drove home in our own car. We'd talked about it and from now on we'd just take one car and share the driving. I liked that idea.

"So what are you going to do now?" he asked.

"Well, I don't know. It's a nice day, we could go down to the river and fish for a while."

"I don't have a license."

"We can stop and get one, they sell them at the bait shop."

"Do you have extra poles?"

"I've got everything we need," I said.

"Let's change and I'll drive," he said.

I changed into my shorts that I wore mowing and a sleeveless tee shirt. I put on my flip-flops and grabbed two fishing poles and my tackle box. Evan was sitting in the car waiting. I put the stuff in back and got in.

Wow. He was wearing gym shorts, pretty short and his dick was obvious in them. On top he had on a tank top and it looked fabulous. It was pale yellow and looked amazing against his dark smooth skin.

"So where do we go?"

I directed him to the bait shop and then to the river. We drove down a sand road to a spot where people fished off the bank. There was one other car and we saw an old man and old woman sitting on stools downriver from the parking spot.

"Let's go up river," I said.

We walked the trail along the riverbank. I found a spot that looked good and we sat on the grass.

"Have you fished in a river before?" I asked.

He grinned.

"The last time I fished my pole had a Mickey Mouse bobber and we fished in a little pond for sunfish."

"I'll rig you up."

I rigged his pole for river fishing and baited it up with a night crawler. I threw the line out because I figured he probably didn't know how to do it. I handed him the pole.

"Hold this for a minute and I'll get us a couple of pole holders."

I broke a branch off a tree and cut two Y shaped sticks and shoved the bottom of each into the riverbank. I put one in front of Evan. I was lower on the bank than he was sitting and I could see up his shorts leg and see his cock and balls. Oh man. His cock looked about three inches or maybe four inches soft and his balls were about the size of walnuts. He had a thick black bush above them.

I didn't dare look too long.

"Here lay your pole in this Y so it stays out of the dirt and we can watch for a bite."

I was a little flustered after seeing his cock. I rigged up my pole and baited it and threw it out. Then I sat down beside him.

"So now we wait," he said giving me a ten thousand watt smile.

"Yup. Fishing is 97% waiting and 3% catching."

He lay back on the grass and raised his arms up over his head. His armpits were beautiful with thick tufts of black hair in them. I could see his left nipple at the edge of his tank top. His cock was obvious in his cotton shorts.

"So you got a girlfriend?" he asked.

"Not right now," I said.

"You had one?"

"Well I had one in high school. But right now with college and everything I just don't seem to have time. How about you?"

"Me either. I had a few girlfriends in high school and college but girls seem to be so hard to get along with. So much drama all the time."

"Oh hell yeah. You've got that right," I said.

I lay back next to him. It was a beautiful day and I loved being with this beautiful boy. We lay there for a while and I heard something rattling. I looked up and Evan's pole was bouncing.

"You've got one!" I yelled.

He sat up and grabbed the pole. The fish was running and pulling line off the reel. He tried to hand it to me.

"Here, take it I'll fuck it up. I've never caught a big fish."

"No way it's your line. Just take your time, I'll coach you."

I told him when to pull and when to let up and after five or six minutes he had about a ten-pound carp flopping in the shallow water. I took off my flip-flops and waded in and tossed it up on the grass.

"Holy shit, that's a whale!" he said, his face beaming.

"They're called carp here," I said grinning.

"Yeah, I know. But it's a good one no?"

"It's a dandy."

"What are we going to do with it?"

"Well they're not very good to eat. Maybe we can just put it back."

"Cool."

I took the fish off and then I grabbed my phone. I handed the fish to Evan and took a picture of him. Then he let it into the water. It lay there for a minute and then it swam off.

"Nice," he said smiling.

"Good job," I said.

He grabbed me and hugged me.

"Thanks for taking me fishing Jake. That was something I'll always remember."

Oh fuck. I'll take you fishing every day if you hug me like that Evan.

We fished for two hours and Evan caught four more fish. None was as big as the first but he had a ball. I managed two small ones.

"So who's the best fisherman now?" he teased on the way home.

"Beginner's luck," I said.

"Oh bull. I'm just more talented. I've got the touch."

"You're pretty cute... for an insane person," I said.

He grinned at me.

"You think I'm cute?"

"A figure of speech," I said.

He nodded.

"Well, for the record, I think you're cute."

I looked over at him and he looked serious.

"Well thanks I guess," I said feeling my face flush.

Thankfully we were home so we both hurried to our houses for dinner. I just got there in time.

"Where have you been Honey?" my mom asked.

"Evan and I went fishing," I said.

"He sure is a nice looking boy. I'm glad you and he are becoming friends."

"You should go over and meet his parents and invite them for a cookout or something," I said.

My dad nodded.

"You're right Jake, we've talked about that. I think we'll go over after dinner and invite them over tomorrow night for some brats on the grill."

Cool, I could spend more time with Evan.

I finished and offered to help with the dishes but my mom said to go that she'd take care of it. I went up to my room and looked across to see if Evan was in his room. He must have still been eating. So I took off my clothes and went to the shower. I picked up my highlighter on the way.

It didn't take long for me to get boned up thinking of looking up Evan's shorts leg and seeing his cock and balls. My dick was hard as hell and I stuck the highlighter in my butt and began jacking off. I had an incredible orgasm and shot cum all over the shower wall. Man I liked that "in the butt" idea.

I dried off and walked out into my bedroom. I looked across the space between the houses and saw Evan's clothes strewn on his bed. His shorts and his shirt were there so he was probably in the shower. My cock started growing.

Shit I felt like a pervert but I wanted to see him naked. I sat next to the window just behind the curtain on a chair and slowly played with my now hard boner. It didn't take long and Evan came out of the shower with his towel wrapped around his waist.

Oh man he had a perfect body. His pectorals were well defined without looking over muscled. His stomach was flat and he had a nice six-pack. My hand sped up.

He took his towel off and dried his hair. His back was to me and I looked at the most perfect ass I'd ever seen. His butt cheeks were perfect bubbles and there was muscle tone to it so it looked like he could crack a walnut in his crack. Then he turned and I almost fell off my chair.

His pubes were thick and black but looked trimmed. His balls hung down and were hairless so I figured he did trim for sure. His cock was beautiful. It was about 4 inches soft, hanging down a little to the left. He was circumcised and it was a luscious light brown color. Then I nearly shit myself. He bent over and dried his legs. His ass cheeks came apart and I could see his asshole. He definitely shaved because there wasn't a hair in it.

My cock began shooting its second load of cum in less than ten minutes. I gasped pretty loud and Evan turned and looked toward my room. I sat still behind the curtain. He looked for a minute and then shook his cock in his hand and walked to the dresser and got a pair of boxers.

I was trapped behind the curtain. Shit.

I sat there with cum dripping off my hand and cock. Then I figured I'd get down on the floor and sneak over to my bathroom door. I slid onto the floor and low-crawled across the floor to the bathroom. Then I got up and washed off my dick and hand and dried them. Then I sauntered out of the bathroom like nothing was amiss.

I looked out of the corner of my eye and saw Evan doing something with his phone. Shit I hoped he'd have seen me naked.

I stood there for a minute and then I coughed loudly. I didn't look at him but looked into my mirror. He turned and looked and saw me naked. He didn't turn away. I took my time looking for boxers and even stroked my cock a little. I watched him in the mirror and he had his hand in his boxers playing with himself. Holy shit… Evan might be a player.

I finally picked some boxers and put them on. Then I turned and Evan was facing away from my window.

"Hey, what's up?" I said across the gap.

He turned and looked surprised. He should be an actor.

"Oh hi, how was your dinner?"

"Good, yours?"

"My mom's not the best cook."

I laughed.

"Don't let her hear you say that."

He shrugged.

"I think my folks are coming over to invite you to a cookout tomorrow."

"Cool, I'll get edible food for a change."

"Evan, don't say things like that about your mom."

"Wait till you taste her food."

I laughed. Damn I wanted to jump across and hug his nearly naked body.

"Well, I'll drive to work tomorrow," I said.

"Okay I'll be ready at quarter to nine."

I went to my TV and turned it on and he did the same. I had no idea what I was watching. All I could think about was Evan and how much I wanted him.

The next morning Evan was waiting by my car when I got to the driveway.

"Hey boss," I said.

"Don't do that," he said. "I'd rather be your friend than your boss."

"I was just kidding. By the way how is it that you just show up from California and you're suddenly the assistant manager?"

"I worked in a Taco Bell in California for the last four years. I started when I was a kid…like you."

"Oh kiss my ass. I've got three pounds of swingin dick and a bucket of balls and you call me kid?"

He laughed and slugged me in the arm playfully.

"Let's go Big Dick," he said.

We headed to the job. We talked about another fishing trip and our cookout that night.

"Oh hey, my folks are getting a swimming pool," he said.

"They're gonna dig a hole in the ground?"

"No nothing that fancy. They're getting an above the ground pool and then there will be a deck around it. It looks nice on the brochure."

"Cool you'll have to invite your fishing instructor over for a swim."

"No doubt. Maybe we can skinny dip some day."

I looked over and he was grinning…evilly.

At work we seemed to be together a lot. He assigned me to jobs that involved him too. We often had to get past each other in the kitchen, which involved a little touch and it seemed that it happened often. I'd sneak a glance at him now and then and many of the times he was glancing at me at the same time. Something was happening to us.

We got home and both went to our rooms to shower. His parents were in my back yard already. I hurried out of the shower without using my highlighter and he was just coming out of his bathroom… naked. He glanced my way and saw my naked body and I saw him. We both stood there looking for half a minute and then we both grinned and got dressed.

"What the hell? I think Evan likes me."

I dressed and headed for the back yard.

"Don't fuck this up. Maybe he's just real friendly. Don't make some stupid move and fuck the whole friendship up. Be cool," I thought to myself.

The parents were having a great time. Julio, Evan's dad had made a pitcher of Margaritas and they were enjoying them. Evan, being over 21 was legal to drink and since I was at my own home I was too. We both poured a drink and sat down with the parents and began talking and telling stories.

"Your Jake he has made my son a fine fisherman," Julio said.

"But Papa, the fish I caught were not the kind you eat," Evan said.

"No matter. Fishing is a noble activity. Give a man a fish and you feed him for a day. Teach a man to fish and …" he couldn't remember the rest.

"He will bring home a fish that you have to clean," his mom said.

We all laughed and Evan looked at me and winked. Damn he was cute.

We had a heck of a good time and the parents got a little tipsy. Evan and I each had two drinks and we were in pretty good shape. I didn't normally drink much and he said he didn't either so we just got pretty relaxed. The old folks retired to their bedrooms and Evan and I decided to stay and sit on a couple of lounges and enjoy the night for a while.

We were sitting side-by-side looking up at the stars. The drinks had made us very mellow and it was very romantic sitting there in the dark.

"That was fun," I said. "I'm glad our folks are getting along. It's nice."

"Yeah, I'm glad too. I knew if your folks were like you it would work. You're a damn good guy Jake."

I looked at him. In the moonlight his skin looked like it was glowing. He was wearing white shorts and a light blue tank top. When he smiled his white teeth nearly glowed. He'd kicked off his sandals and was sitting barefoot as was I.

We sat there for a minute and then he took my hand in his.

"Jake I like you."

My hand was trembling.

"I like you too Evan."

He squeezed my hand. Then he leaned over toward my chair. I leaned toward him and our lips met. We had a quick kiss. We broke it and stared into each other's eyes from an inch away.

"Jake I don't want to make a mistake here."

"You're not making a mistake. I want this too."

We kissed again and this time our tongues were in each other's mouths. Our hands were roaming and we were groping each other's cocks.

"We can't do this here," I whispered.

"Where?"

"Let's sneak up to my room. My parents sleep like they're dead when they've had some drinks."

We got up and I took his hand and we snuck up to my room. We went in and I shut the door. My heart was pounding.

"Jake are you sure about this?"

"I wanted you from the first day when I saw you carrying furniture," I said.

We wrapped our arms around each other and began making out. Man he was a good kisser. Then he took my shirt off over my head and raised his arms so I could take his off. I pulled it over his head and put my mouth on his left nipple and began sucking it.

"Oh fuck," he whispered.

I sucked both nipples and then he sucked on mine making my cock throb. We kissed some more and then he pulled my shorts down. My cock sprang out. He looked at it and smiled.

"Nice," he said. He dropped to his knees and licked the tip. It was wet with precum. Then he took it in his mouth and sucked on it. I closed my eyes and gritted my teeth. I was afraid I'd cum right away and didn't want to.

"Evan, slow down or I'll cum," I said.

He stood up smiling. He looked down at the front of his shorts. It was obvious he had a boner.

I pulled his shorts down and it sprang up. Oh man it was a beauty. Mine is six inches exactly. I measured. His was at least an inch longer and it stood up like a little brown soldier in front of his pubic bush.

I knelt down and took it in my hand. It felt like it was on fire. I pulled it down so I could get it in my mouth. There was a big drop of precum on the end and I licked that off. Then I took about half of his dick into my mouth and began sucking him. He moaned and groaned.

"Evan, shhhh."

"Sorry," he giggled. "Let's lay on the bed I want to suck you too."

We went to the bed and got in a 69. We both went to work on the other's cock and it didn't take long and I knew the end was in sight for me. I felt the feeling and said, "Evan I'm close."

"Me too, I want to swallow it."

"Okay I want to also."

We sucked for another minute and then I felt my balls clench up and I came in his mouth. He milked my cock with his lips and got every drop. His cock twitched and filled my mouth with hot cum a second later. I took his cock head in my lips and sucked on it like a lollipop.

"Oh fuck, oh man," he gasped.

He finally quit shooting and we both lay on our backs side-by-side on the bed. We were both panting and sweating. I got up and grabbed a towel and wiped his face off and then wiped mine off. I lay down next to him and smiled at him.

"That was wonderful," I said as I leaned over and kissed him.

"I'm so glad," he said. "I was afraid to say something or do something. I had a crush on you from the first day I saw you."

"I felt the same way Evan. Damn if we weren't such chicken shits we could have been sucking each other off for a week."

He laughed. 'We've got all summer," he said.

We kissed a few more times and then he dressed and I put on my boxers. I snuck downstairs with him and we kissed at the back door.

"See you in the morning," I said.

"I'm looking forward to it," he said. He kissed me once more and sprinted across the yard and went into his house.

I don't think my feet touched the stairs as I went up to bed. The room smelled like sex and I lay there inhaling his scent.

"Damn," I thought to myself. "I think I'm falling in love."

Evan was waiting in his car for me when I jogged out the front door. I felt like a million dollars after our first sexual encounter the night before.

I got in and turned to him.

"Hey good looking," I said.

He smiled cautiously.

"Hi Jake, ready to go?"

Uh oh.

We pulled out on the street and headed toward Taco Bell. I knew something was wrong and hated to say anything but I had to.

"Evan what's wrong?"

"I'm just feeling… I'm," he stammered.

"Are you having second thoughts about last night?"

"Jake I don't want to take advantage of you," he said.

"Evan you,"

"Jake let me say this… please."

I shut up.

"When I lived in California I found that I was attracted to guys. I fought it for a long time and finally gave in when I met a guy on the beach. He came onto me and I couldn't fight the attraction and we ended up having sex. We became boyfriends and I was going to move in with him when we had a fight about some stupid thing. He kicked me out and shortly afterward my parents told me we were moving. So when I got here I thought I'd make a new start and try to fight the feelings I have for guys. It didn't work."

"Evan I have feelings for you too."

"Jake I seduced you. I had no right to do that. I feel like a pervert coming on to a younger guy who had no idea what he was getting into."

"Evan, I'm only a little over two years younger and you're not the first guy I've had sex with."

He looked surprised.

"What?"

"Evan I've always felt like you did. I always had an attraction to other guys but I fought it too. I dated girls and had sex with several of them. But each time it left me unsatisfied. I got more satisfaction jacking off with the face of a cute boy in my mind than actually fucking a girl. So you're not seducing me at all. If anything I stalked you."

"You're serious? Jake you've been with other guys?"

"Just two and it was just a few weeks ago at school. They were my best two friends and we somehow went from being friends to being friends who had sex with each other. They're a couple now I think."

"So what we did was okay for you?"

"Oh Evan, I don't think I've ever had a sexual experience that was more wonderful than that first kiss from you or tasting your beautiful cock for the first time."

He blinked a few times and a tear ran down his cheek.

"Jake you can't know how that makes me feel. It was a great experience for me too. I was terrified when I touched your hand but I was so attracted to you I had to try it.

I took his hand in mine and kissed it.

"Evan I want us to be together."

"Me too."

We were at the restaurant so we parked and he shut off the car. There was no one in the parking lot. He grinned and leaned over and we had a kiss.

"That'll have to hold us until after work," he said.

"Damn I'm gonna be sporting a boner all day."

We got out and walked to the door.

"I'll have to put you in the kitchen today then. We can't have your big cock sticking out in front of your uniform and scaring all the little old ladies half to death."

I swallowed hard. Damn how fucking lucky was I.

Later in the day Evan posted the work schedule for the next week. I looked and saw that he and I both had off the next day.

"So it's just a coincidence you scheduled us both off tomorrow?" I said grinning.

"I thought we might go fishing again."

"And then?"

"Maybe a little hot naked sex at the river," he said quietly.

"Oh man," I said. We were in the back hall where the mops and stuff were stored. I checked to see if anyone was around and then I groped his crotch. He grinned.

"Stop that!"

"I love that thing," I said.

"Stop it, I'll get hard and then what the hell will I do?"

I made a jacking motion with my hand.

"No I'm saving that for after work. I want your mouth to do that."

"Oh boy."

"Drive faster," I said.

"I'll get a speeding ticket."

"I'll pay for it," I said.

Evan grinned at me.

"Your house or mine?"

"Yours, I want to see where you live."

We ran from the car to the house. His parents were at work so we didn't even slow down. We sprinted up the stairs and to his bedroom. I was taking off my clothes as he locked the door. I was down to my socks and stripped them off and then began tearing his clothes off. We were both naked in less than a minute.

We wrapped our arms around each other and began making out. Our hard cocks were mashing together and I could feel wetness on them. We moved toward the bed with our mouths together and our arms around each other. When we got close we fell on the bed. Evan wrapped his legs around me and rolled onto his back. I began humping him. He was sucking my tongue so hard it hurt.

"Oh Jake, oh damn," he panted.

I nibbled on his earlobe and then stuck my tongue into his ear. He giggled when I did that. Then I kissed his neck and kissed each eyelid. He had his hands on my back and ass and gently stroked them as I kissed him all over. I went down to his nipples and sucked on them until they both stood up like little Hershey kisses. Then I went down and stuck my tongue into his belly button.

"Oh fuck, suck me Jake or I'm gonna explode," he stammered.

I moved down to his crotch. It was magnificent. His balls hung low and loose and I licked his sack. Then I took each of his balls into my mouth and sucked on them. I licked under his ball sack and then I licked his cock from the stem to the head.

"Oh fuck," he whispered.

"I grasp his cock in my hand. The damn thing was hard as a baseball bat. I pulled up on it so I could get it in my mouth. The tip was shiny with precum and I licked it off like a popsickle. I put the head in my mouth and went down about three inches on his cock. It was so thick that it was about all I could do to take that much.

I sucked on his cock head and swirled my tongue around it.

"Oh Jake, I'm gonna cum," he said.

"Cum for me baby," I said.

I'd just gotten my mouth over his head when it started shooting squirts of hot cum. Evan shook all over as his cock exploded into my mouth. I milked it with my hand and worked a hell of a lot of cum out of it. Then I licked it from end to end, kissed his balls and lay back down next to him. He put his arms around me and we kissed.

"Oh Jake, that was beautiful."

"You're beautiful Evan. You're the most beautiful boy I've ever known."

He put his face next to my neck and hugged me so hard one of my vertebrae cracked. We started laughing.

"Jeez you broke my back!" I said.

"Oh shit. Are you paralyzed?"

"If I am you'll have to jack me off for the rest of my life."

"Damn will your dick still work?"

I reached down and stroked it.

"I believe it's okay," I said.

"Well then…"

We kissed a few times and then he sucked my left nipple. He bit it and it hurt a little but was really erotic too. When that one was hard he did the right one too. Then he licked my belly button and fondled my balls.

"Lick my balls," I whispered.

He lifted my sack up and slurped one then the other into his mouth.

"Oh fuck that feels naughty," I said.

I could feel his tongue running over each of my balls. Then he let them drop out of his mouth and he licked my sack down to my butt crack. He fingered my hole and then took my dick head in his mouth.

"Oh Evan, I'm close get on it," I said urgently.

He got about two inches of my cock in his mouth and I started squirting. I came so hard my balls hurt. He sucked on my dick head and worked his tongue around it until I stopped cumming. Then he milked a few last drops out of it and lay down next to me.

I was panting from the excitement.

"Holy shit, I thought my balls were going to fall off, I came so hard," I panted.

He laughed and hugged me.

"Damn I love you Jake."

We both stopped for a second. I looked into his beautiful brown eyes.

"Do you really Evan?"

He nodded.

"I do… I love you Jake."

I pulled him to me. I hugged him hard.

"I love you too Evan. I've never been in love before but I am now. I love you so fucking much."

We lay there in each other's arms and we both had tears in our eyes. I lay my head against his chest and the next thing I knew I heard someone talking downstairs.

"Evan! Wake up. Your parents are home!"

He woke with a start.

"What? Holy fuck!"

We got up and scrambled to get dressed. Clothes were strewn all over the place so we had to find them first. We just finished dressing and were looking for our sneakers when his mom knocked on the door.

"Evan is Jake in there with you?"

"Yeah Mom, why?"

"His parents are coming over for dinner. His mother just wasn't sure where he was."

"I'm here. I'm going to run home and change. We were playing a video game," I lied.

"That's fine Jake. I'll tell her. Oh by the way I'm glad you and Evan have become friends. It's nice that you two get along so well."

She had no idea.

I ran home and went to the shower. I stripped off my clothes and began laughing. I was wearing Evan's boxers. I went out to my room and to the window naked. He was getting undressed and he looked surprised when he was he had on the wrong boxers too.

"Looking for these?" I said quietly.

He turned and laughed. He took his dick and wagged it at me.

"See you in a bit," he said.

I blew him a kiss.

My folks and I walked across the yard to the neighbor's patio. Evan was there with his dad. Evan was wearing loose shorts and a tank top and barefoot. I had on some gym shorts and a tee and was wearing sandals, which I kicked off when we got there. Evan's dad had a pitcher of Gin-coolers made and offered us one. We all had one of the drinks. Evan and I both grinned as we tasted the lemony stuff.

"Like drinking lemon soda," I said.

"I will kick you in the butt if you drink too much," my dad said.

"Not me. I don't like hangovers," I said.

"Jacob when have you had a hangover? You're not old enough to drink," my mom said.

"Mom, I'm in college. We don't drink sodas and energy drinks all the time. I don't party much but I'm not a prude."

Evan was enjoying it.

His mom brought out a tray with food on it. Evan looked at me and made a face.

"Be careful," he whispered. "Don't take too much."

How bad could it be? It looked pretty nice.

We sat at the table and passed the dishes around. When I put the first forkful in my mouth I must have looked surprised. Evan snorted and nearly choked.

"What's wrong dear?" his mom asked.

"Nothing Mom... just went down the wrong pipe."

I didn't know what the food was but I knew Evan was right. It was not good. Not by any trick of the imagination could I find it edible.

I could tell my folks thought the same thing.

"This is an old Danish recipe," Evan's mom said.

"Interesting," my mom replied.

"Pass the bread," Evan said.

We ate and forced the stuff down. I ate a lot of bread. Evan's dad filled our drinks and I realized my dad was right. I felt a little warm in the face.

The parents were talking and I felt something on my foot. I looked across the table and Evan was grinning. He had his bare foot on mine rubbing it.

I smiled at him and he moved it up my leg. I smiled even more.

Then he lifted his foot up and I felt his toes sliding into the leg of my shorts. I must have looked surprised because he giggled.

Then the horny shit put his foot up my shorts leg until his toes were rubbing against my balls. I felt my dick beginning to move.

"Stop."

I mouthed the word.

He shook his head.

"Stop it!"

He grinned. I reached down under the table and grabbed his big toe and twisted it. It made a cracking sound and he yelped.

"What's wrong Evan?" his mom asked.

"I got a cramp," he said pulling his foot back.

"Eat more bananas," my dad said.

After dinner Evan and I walked over to my house telling the folks we were going to play my new Playstation game.

When we got to my house we went to the kitchen and found a plate of cold chicken and some cake. We took it upstairs.

"Let's get naked," Evan said.

"Jeez what a horny shit."

"Come on, get naked."

I didn't have to be asked three times. We both stripped down and sat cross-legged on my bed and ate chicken and cake.

"Damn you were right," I said.

"About my mom's cooking?"

I nodded.

"What the hell was that stuff?"

"I have no idea. I don't think she really has a recipe. She just puts stuff together until it fills the pot. My dad and I have lived off Hot Pockets for years."

I laughed and leaned over and kissed him with my greasy mouth.

"Damn you're cute when you're covered with grease," I said. "Let's shower together."

"Now? What about our folks?"

Evan jumped up and snuck to the window. He came back holding his cock.

"They're making another pitcher of drinks. They won't be back for a while and when they do come back they won't even think about us."

He cocked his head off to the side and gave me a little smirk. Then he jacked his dick a few times.

"Who wants more desert?"

We sprinted to the bathroom giggling like a couple of twelve year-old girls. Since we were already naked we got the water running and then got in. We both were hard as hell already and we soaped each other up and then caressed and fondled each other for a long time. We hugged and kissed and ran our fingers up each other's ass cracks.

"Oh Jake, this is amazing," Evan said. "I want us to do this forever."

"Me too gorgeous. I love everything about you."

"My cock hurts. We've got to cum or I'm going to have a stroke."

"Let's 69," I said.

We got out of the shower and dried each other off. Then we walked hand-in-hand to my bed. Evan lay with his head at the top of the bed and I lay with mine at the bottom. We took each other's cocks in our mouths and began sucking each other. I licked Evan's balls and he lifted up his leg. I moved down and licked that part of him that wasn't balls and wasn't asshole.

"Oh Jake," he whispered.

He shuddered when I licked him there. That turned me on and I licked his pretty little pink asshole. It was sweet and clean and putting my tongue on it was very erotic.

"Jake, oh man," he gasped.

"You like that?"

"Oh fuck that feels so amazing."

I lapped at his hole for a long time. I used my hand to jack him slowly as I licked him.

"Jake I'm gonna cum," he said urgently.

I put his cock in my mouth and put my finger on his asshole and pushed it in. He erupted in my mouth with a flood of cum. His ass muscle clenched on my finger and he made a hell of a lot of noise moaning.

"Jeez, not so loud," I said laughing.

"Holy fuck, that really set me off," he said panting.

"You like?"

"Fucking right I like. Where did you learn that?"

"It just looked so nice I wanted to lick it."

"Damn."

I rolled over on my back and he knelt between my legs. He took my cock back in his mouth and bean sucking me. Then he did the same thing I'd done. He moved to my balls and then to my ass crack. I lifted up my legs and he lapped at my asshole. His tongue felt incredible licking it and probing into it.

"Oh fuck Evan, that does feel good."

"Mmmm."

He jacked me while he ate my ass and it didn't take long for me to get the feeling.

"Evan it won't be long," I said.

He kept licking my ass.

"Evan hurry!"

He raised his head and opened his mouth to put my cock in it and I shot cum. The first squirt went right up on his forehead and then he got over it and sucked the rest from it. When I was finished he lay beside me.

I began laughing.

"You've got cum all over your face," I said.

"Lick it off," he said with a wicked look on his face.

I grinned and stuck my tongue out. I licked the cum off him and then licked his face all over. When I had him all wet he opened his mouth and sucked on my tongue.

We lay there resting. He looked at me and smiled.

"What a perfect boyfriend," he said.

"I'm the luckiest guy in the world," I said.

We lay there naked in each other's arms and it was dark when I woke. The parents were not on the patio so I figured they were gone to bed. I looked at Evan lying there next to me. He was so handsome and such a prefect boy. My heart felt full of love for him. I pulled a blanket over us and went back to sleep next to my naked lover.

"What time is it?" Evan asked.

I opened my eyes to see my perfect lover sitting on the bed next to me. I looked at my alarm clock on the dresser.

"It's a little after nine."

"Shit we're late for work."

"Evan we have the day off... remember?"

"Oh shit yeah. Damn I about shit when I woke up next to you. Do you suppose our parents knew?"

"I doubt it. They were a little full when they got done with their drinks and mine never talk to me in the morning. They get up and they're off to work."

"Mine too. They probably never knew we spent the night together."

"It was nice sleeping with you," I said.

"Yeah, real nice."

"Let's have a shower and then have some breakfast."

We got up and walked naked to the bathroom. I gave Evan a toothbrush from a box of them we kept in the vanity. We stood side-by-side brushing our teeth and then we checked our chins. I didn't have much of a beard but I could use a shave. Evan's beard was much heavier and with his dark hair it was more noticeable, so we both lathered up and shaved. Even something as simple as shaving was very sexy standing next to him watching his dick swing as he moved.

We got in the shower and washed each other's hair and than washed each other's bodies. We boned up when we washed each other's cocks and balls.

"Umm, that feels good," Evan said as I stroked his cock.

"Let's save it until after breakfast," I said.

"Well then you better take your hand off it or it'll spit on you," he said.

We finished and dried off and went to the kitchen naked.

I put on one of Mom's aprons and began frying bacon and eggs. Evan made toast and set the table and got the orange juice and milk out.

"You look so... domestic," he said grinning.

I wiggled my ass.

"Senor, you like my caboose?"

He grinned and walked up behind me. He wrapped his arms around me and I felt his cock in my butt crack.

"I like it," he whispered in my ear.

"After breakfast," I said.

We ate with gusto. After the dinner his mom had made we were hungry and of course a night of sex made us hungry too. We cleaned up the kitchen and walked hand-in-hand upstairs.

We went to my bed and embraced and began kissing. Both of us were hard.

"Evan I want you to make love to me," I said.

"You mean do IT?"

"Yes I want you to fuck me."

"Are you sure? It's a big step."

"Evan I love you. I want to show you my love by making love to you."

He kissed me hard.

"I'd love to," he said.

I went to my dresser and dug under my socks and came back with a condom and a tube of lube.

"You just happened to have that?" he said grinning.

"It's a leftover from my days of dating girls. I hope it's not all dried out."

I tore open the foil and the condom was fine. I leaned down and sucked his cock for a minute and then rolled it down over him. I squirted some lube on my hand and jacked him to get it slippery.

Then I put some lube in my ass.

"How do you want to do it?" I asked.

"I want to face you so I can see your beautiful face," he said quietly.

I kissed him and lay on my back on the bed. He knelt between my legs. I lifted them up and held onto my knees and pulled my ass up for him.

"Oh Jake," he said.

He leaned over me and took one hand and guided his big thick cock to my asshole. I closed my eyes and gritted my teeth. I knew it was going to hurt. He put the head against my hole and pushed. I moaned and he backed off.

"Go ahead, don't mind me," I said.

"Jake I don't want to hurt you."

"I'm okay Evan, do it."

He pushed again and the head slid in. Oh man. I groaned and he stopped.

"Go slow my love," I said.

He went slowly and gently and in a couple of minutes his pubes were brushing my balls. My ass felt full and the pain turned to pleasure.

"Oh Evan that's amazing. Make love to me."

He took his time and fucked me slowly. He was gentle and loving. As we fucked he leaned down and we kissed and he sucked my nipples. I wrapped my legs around him and watched his gorgeous face as he pushed his big cock into me.

We must have fucked for ten minutes or more when Evan began making a noise deep in his chest.

"I'm close Jake."

"Cum in me my love," I said leaning up and kissing him.

We had our mouths on each other kissing when I felt his cock throbbing. I knew he was filling the condom with cum. He pushed into me as far as he could go and held it there. It throbbed and finally stopped. We laid there panting and kissing, sweat dripping off us.

"God, that was the most erotic thing I've ever done," he said.

"Evan I love you," I said.

He kissed me deeply. "I love you too Jake."

His cock began to soften and he pulled it out. The condom was half full of cum.

He pulled it off is cock and held it up.

"Pour it on my cock and jack me off with it," I said.

He grinned.

"Kinky."

He turned the condom over and his hot cum ran out onto my boner. Then he took it in his hand and began jacking me off. I closed my eyes and enjoyed the sensation of the wetness of his cum and his hot hand. It didn't take long.

"Oh fuck Evan, I'm nearly there," I said.

Then he surprised me. He leaned down and put my cock in his mouth and sucked me until I came. He swallowed my cum and licked his cum off my cock. Then he lay on top of me and kissed me.

"I can taste our cum," I said.

"I love the taste of your cum Jake."

We wrapped our arms around each other and lay there resting. If I died right that moment my life would have been fulfilled.

"Evan how did I ever live before I met you?" I said.

"I was just thinking the same thing."

"I want us to be together from now on," I said.

"I do too Jake. We're going to have to figure that out. But right now, let's take a shower and decide what to do with the rest of our day off."

We ran to the shower and had a lovely wash, with a lot of kissing.

Evan wanted to go fishing again. I guess I'd created not only a new lover but also a new fishing buddy. We got bait and went to the river where we'd gone before. There were three groups fishing on the bank. The same old couple was there and there was an old man with what looked like his grandson and a teenage boy and a teenage girl.

We set up using our old pole holders, kicked off our flip-flops and took off our shirts. We'd brought a blanket along and we lay back on it and watched for a bite. It was a perfect day. It was nice and warm without being hot and there was a nice breeze. I looked over at Evan and he was staring intently at his pole. The breeze was making the hair in his armpits ruffle and it looked sexy as hell.

"I love your armpit hair," I said.

He grinned.

"You do? I was thinking of shaving it off."

"Oh fuck no. It's sexy as hell. I like your bush too."

"It needs trimming," he said.

"You trim?"

"Yeah, otherwise I'd look like a fucking bear."

"I think I could use a little trim."

He got an evil grin on his face.

"Maybe we can trim each other up."

I felt my cock twitch.

"Yeah that sounds like fun," I said.

Evan jumped up and grabbed his pole and set the hook into a fish. He fought it like a pro and landed a nice catfish. I helped him get it off the hook with my pliers and we let it go.

"The fishing pro strikes again," he said.

"Jeez. I've created a monster."

The afternoon wore on. We caught a fish every so often and had a great time. One by one our neighbors left, leaving just us alone on the riverbank.

"All alone," I said.

Evan turned and looked at me.

"All alone in a lovely setting out in nature and here we are."

I grinned.

"Did you happen to bring one of those condoms?"

He reached in his pocket and held one up.

"My motto, Be Prepared."

"Want to?"

He nodded.

"I want you to do me," he said.

"Really? Mine is pretty fat," I said.

"I'm ready for it Jake. It's all I've thought about since this morning when I did it to you. I want to try it. And if I'm going to do it I want it to be with the guy I love."

We rolled together and began kissing. It didn't take long and we both were hard and the next thing we knew we were naked and Evan was rolling the condom down my cock.

"Damn it barely goes on. We're going to have to get some Magnums for that big thing," he said.

"Did you bring the lube?"

"No, I'll lube your dick and you can lube my ass."

He knelt over my dick and slurped on it with his mouth and got it all full of spit. Then he stood up and backed up to my face and bent over and spread his ass cheeks. There was his beautiful hole in my face. I stuck my face in between his cheeks and lapped as his pucker making it all wet and slippery.

"I want to be on my back like you did," he said.

He lay down and lifted his legs. I got between them and held my cock and put it up to his pucker. He looked a little scared.

"Evan we don't have to."

"Do it," he said.

I put my dick head to his hole and pushed. He moaned loudly but the damn thing went in. I stopped because my dick began to throb.

"Oh fuck, hold still."

"What's wrong?"

"I almost came when it went in. Whew that was almost the shortest fuck in history."

He smiled at me and I pushed in and then pulled back and in a minute I was all the way inside him.

"Oh man, that's a load," he said.

"Are you okay?"

"I'm great. It's feeling better now. Make love to me Jakey."

Evan wrapped his legs around me and we fucked like we'd done it all our lives. We kissed and he pinched my nipples and ass and it was like being in heaven. After many minutes I felt my cock getting that feeling.

"I'm about to cum Evan," I said.

"Pull out and shoot it on my face," he said.

I grinned.

"Really?"

"Yeah," he said taking his own cock in his hand and starting to jack himself off.

"Kinky," I said grinning.

I stroked into him about three more times and then pulled out and ripped the condom off. I walked forward on my knees and he lifted up his head and opened his mouth. I jacked myself and shot cum all over his face and into his mouth. He was jacking himself furiously and I turned around and lay my face by his cock. He began shooting and shot cum all over my face and chest. Then I took it in my mouth and milked the last of it from him.

We both lay there panting. I turned around and we kissed. Both of us were covered with cum.

"How was that?" I asked.

"Wow," he said.

We lay there in the sun resting. I heard a clunk sound.

We looked up and a canoe was going past with two guys in it.

"Nice day," one said.

"Um yeah," I said.

I looked at Evan and he broke out laughing.

"You know, right now I don't give a shit who knows. I love you Jake."

"Me either Evan. I want the world to know. I love Evan."

After a while we got up and waded into the river and washed the cum off our bodies. We reeled up our fishing poles and went back to the car.

"I'm not sure how I lived before I met you," I said.

He leaned over and kissed me.

"I was thinking the same thing."

The next day when Evan and I got home from work the pool had arrived and the workers who were installing it had made a lot of progress. The pool itself was up and looked finished. It was about twenty feet across and five feet deep. They had trenches dug in the yard for pipes and electricity and there was a pile of treated lumber that would become a deck the next day or two.

"That'll be nice," I said.

"We can swim in the evening when the folks have gone to bed."

I grinned at him.

"Yeah and?"

"We'll think of something."

We both went home to shower. I resisted the urge to jack off in the shower just in case Evan wanted to mess around later. When I got out and walked into my room he was at his window naked.

"My mom is cooking," he said just loudly enough for me to hear.

I shrugged.

"Invite me to go downtown for pizza…please?"

I laughed.

"You have to promise to fuck me later."

"I promise."

I dressed in some athletic shorts and a tank top, slipped on my flip-flops and walked next door. I knocked and Evan's mom came out.

"I was going for pizza and wanted to see if Evan would like to go with me," I said smiling sweetly.

"Well isn't that nice of you? I am making one of his favorite dishes for dinner but I'll ask him."

She called up to his room and he came down the stairs dressed similarly to me.

"Hey, I'm going for pizza, want to come?"

"Oh wow, Mom is making lutefisk, but sure I hate to see you have to go alone."

"Go on sweetie. I'll save some for you."

We jumped in my car and Evan was smiling from ear to ear.

"What the hell is lutefisk?" I asked.

"Oh God, it's the most awful thing you can imagine. It's codfish that's been soaked in lye and then simmered in water. It looks okay but tastes like fish flavored jello and it stinks like a hot whore's pussy on an August afternoon."

I broke out laughing.

"A hot whore's pussy? Have you smelled many of them?"

My beautiful Evan grinned.

"No but I can imagine. Trust me Jake you do NOT want to eat lutefisk."

"I'll take your word for it."

He reached over and took my hand and put it up to his mouth and kissed it.

"Damn I'm so glad we moved next door to you," he said.

I felt my eyes get wet.

"Evan, my life is so wonderful now, I'm so happy."

We got to the pizza place and took a booth and ordered.

"Jake, what are we going to do when summer is over?"

"I don't know. Every time I think about that I get a sick feeling inside. I don't know if I can go back to being without you."

"You're going back to school at the same place right?"

"Yeah."

"I'm checking into their admissions requirements and it looks like I could transfer there with not much trouble."

I almost jumped up and kissed him.

"You mean we could both be in school together?"

He nodded.

"Oh man that'd be great."

"I was thinking we might get a place and live together," he said.

I thought I was going to cry right in the middle of the pizza place.

"Evan, nothing would make me happier."

I wanted to get up and put my arms around him and make out but thought it might be a bit much in a pizza place full of families.

We were both nearly giddy as we ate pizza and talked about living together. When we got to the car we embraced and kissed.

"Let's go and make love," he said.

I drove like a man possessed. We got to my house and my folks were watching TV.

"We're going to play Zombies Mom," I said as we hurried upstairs.

We went in my room and were naked in less than a minute. I stood looking at this most beautiful boy and my heart nearly burst with love. We embraced and began making out. We worked our way to the bed and I lay on my back and Evan lay on top of me grinding his big cock into mine.

"Evan, have you ever had sex with anyone without a condom?"

"No, I never have. I always used one."

"Me either. I always used one when I was with a girl and when I messed with Todd and Joey we used them too."

"That's good," he said.

"What I'm saying is that if you and I are going to be together and never mess with anyone else, we really don't need one."

He thought about that for a minute.

"You're right. I don't want anyone else Jake. I have the person I want to be with forever."

"I feel the same Evan. I love you more than anything."

"So we should just... do it?"

I grinned.

"Make love to me."

We were getting pretty good at this fucking deal. Evan knew just how to get me worked up by sucking my balls and then sucking my dick and then licking my ass. By the time he lubed up his cock and put it into my hole I was begging for it. I wrapped my arms and legs around him and he fucked me slowly and lovingly. We kissed and sucked on each other's tongues and took our time making love. When he finally got close to cumming I took my cock in my hand and began jacking. It only took a few pulls and I shot cum up on my chest. Evan pushed as deeply as he could go and I felt him shooting inside me. I could imagine his cum in my ass and it was a huge turn-on. He left his cock in me until it got soft and then it slipped out. We lay there panting and sweating and kissing.

"Evan that was lovely," I said.

"I want us to do that for the rest of our lives," he said as he kissed me.

We got up and showered and dressed. We decided to actually play Zombies for a while. My phone began jingling and I answered it. It was Joey.

"Hey limp dick, how's it hangin'?"

"Long and loose and full of juice."

"That fat thing must hold a quart of juice," he said laughing.

"Joey! Hey man it's good to hear your voice. How is summer going?"

"It's great Jake. Todd and I have… well we're a couple now Jake."

"No shit? You're an official couple?"

"Yeah, we came out to our families and it's good. At first they freaked a little but once they got over the shock they're handling it pretty well."

"Wow, that's cool Joey. All because we got blowjobs together?"

He laughed. "I'd been having thoughts about Todd for a while and once we got together I found out that he had feelings for me too. But the blowjobs started the whole thing going so I guess we can thank you for helping with that."

"You guys make a good couple. I'm real happy for you."

"Thanks Jake. Hey what I was calling about is that Todd and I want to get an apartment for the school year and wondered if you'd like to live with us."

"Fuck yeah! That'd be great. But I have a little situation here too."

"What?"

"I've got a boyfriend too Joey."

"No fucking way!"

"Yes way."

I could hear him talking to Todd in the background.

"You've got a boyfriend?" Todd asked.

"Yeah, he moved in next door from California. We started messing around a while ago and now we're in love Todd."

"No way!"

I could hear him telling Joey and I laughed listening to them. They were like an old married couple.

"Well that makes it perfect," Joey said coming back on the phone. "The place we're looking at is two bedrooms. Your guy and you can have one and we'll have the other. He can speak English and stuff can't he?"

"Fuck you Joey. His name is Evan and he's two years ahead of us in school. He's the most beautiful guy I've ever seen and we're fucking each other's brains out."

"Oh man."

He told Todd the whole thing.

"Listen let us talk to our parents about it. How soon do you have to know?"

"We're going to sign the lease next week. Get you and your guy down here and we'll do that and have some fun."

I promised him I'd get back to him in a few days and hung up.

"By listening to that I'm thinking we might have a place to live?" Evan asked.

"We do and with two of the coolest guys you'll ever know."

"Not as cool as you," he said kissing me.

Zombies were forgotten. Clothes were strewn from the couch to the bed and in no time I was making love to Evan. We were wrapped in each other's arms and I was in him fucking his beautiful ass. When I came I let it go inside him and he kissed me deeply as he felt my cock throbbing. I pulled it out and sucked him off and he shot a good load into my throat.

We lay there panting.

"Damn you're wearing me out," he said, with sweat running down his forehead.

"We have to do this. We're at our sexual peak. It's only right that we make as much cum as possible in these peak years," I said.

"Thank you professor. Let's shower, I'm all sweaty."

I kissed him on the lips and then I bent down and kissed his limp dick, just for fun.

The pool was finished. The deck was up and stained and looked really nice. Evan's folks invited us over for a barbeque.

"God, I hope it's hamburgers or hot dogs and not some "Scandanavian Surprise" my dad said."

"Oh my gosh, don't you dare say anything," my mom said.

We lucked out. They had hamburgers and brats and potato salad that she bought at the deli. Evan and I were glowing. We were together and our families were friends. Life was good.

He looked at me and shrugged. I knew he wanted me to bring up the subject of the apartment.

"Hey I almost forgot," I said, "Joey called yesterday and he and Todd, my other buddy from school are getting an apartment this fall and they invited me to share it with them."

"You don't want to live in the dorm?" my mom asked.

"Oh it was okay but it's so noisy. It's hard to study."

"Will it cost the same?" my dad asked.

"I'll make up whatever difference there might be," I said, "In fact, Evan is transferring to the UW and they invited him to share with them too. That way the cost would be split by four of us."

"Evan is that what you want?" his dad asked.

"Yeah, Jake and I are good friends and we'd probably have no trouble getting a part-time job at a Taco Bell there. I think it'd be fun. I don't know these guys but Jake says they're good guys, so I'll take his word for it."

The parents chewed it over and soon we had an okay from them. Evan was beaming.

We sat by the pool for a long time talking and finally the old folks got tired and went to their own homes and to bed. Evan and I sat there holding hands after they left.

"We'll let them get to sleep and then let's go skinny-dipping," Evan said conspiratorially.

I was grinning from ear to ear.

We waited a half hour and there was no sound or lights coming from the houses. We got up and kissed and undressed each other. Evan's body was beautiful in the moonlight. His dark skin actually glowed and his hard-on was glistening on the tip.

I leaned over and licked the precum off. He shuddered.

"Let's get in," he said quietly.

We slipped into the water. It was perfect. We swam noiselessly and then we stopped in the middle and stood with our arms around each other and made out. Evan put his arms around me and wrapped his legs around my waist.

"Make love to me Jakey," he whispered.

I shifted him around so his asshole was right at my cock. Then he reached down and guided it into his ass as I held him. He moved down a little until my whole cock was up his ass.

"Oh God," he gasped.

We went slowly and he moved up and down on me for a long time. We kissed and sucked each other's tongues and after a quarter of an hour I was close.

"I'm going to cum Evan," I said.

He worked up and down another time or two and I began shooting inside him. I could feel his ass muscle clenching my cock.

"Oh Jake, I can feel it," he mumbled.

He put his face against my neck and bit me.

Finally my cock began to shrink and it slipped from his ass.

We kissed passionately.

"That was amazing Evan," I said.

"It was for me too Jake, I love your cock inside me."

We lay back in the water and rested. Evan moved next to me and we held each other.

"You need to cum," I said.

He smiled.

"Make love to me gorgeous," I said.

"I'd love to handsome."

We moved to the side of the pool. I put my arms on the edge of the deck and backed my feet up and spread them apart. Evan walked between my legs and I felt his big cock against my butt cheeks. He ran his finger up my ass and then I felt his dick head probing my crack.

"Can you pull your butt cheeks apart?" he whispered.

I pulled them apart and he put his cock up to my asshole. He pushed and the head went in. I moaned.

"Should I stop?"

"Oh fuck no! That was a moan of delight," I said.

He kissed me on the cheek. Then he began shoving that huge cock up my ass.

"Oh Jake, this is so fucking erotic," he said.

"Fill my ass sweetie," I said.

He pumped my ass for several minutes and then I noticed he picked up his pace.

"Cumming," he panted.

I felt his cock twitching in my ass and knew he was spewing his cum into me. I clenched his dick with my ass muscle and he jumped.

"Oh fuck!" he said quite loudly.

I started laughing

"Shh, you'll wake everybody up," I said giggling.

"Damn that felt like something bit my cock."

"My cock eating ass," I said.

He pulled out of me and we embraced and kissed. Our wet bodies shimmered in the moonlight and it was very sexual and beautiful.

"I love you Evan, more than anything in the world," I whispered.

"I love you too Jake, more than life."

It was a beautiful moment.

A couple of days later Evan and I had the day off again. We decided to go fishing but first Evan wanted me to come over to his house. I got up and slipped on a pair of loose gym shorts and walked barefoot and shirtless to his house. He saw me coming and told me to come up to his room.

I went in and he was naked. I smiled.

"Okay, you want top or bottom?"

He grinned and shook his head.

"Time to trim," he said holding up a little shaver.

I grinned.

"Kinky," I said.

"It'd be easier if you trimmed me and I trimmed you," he said.

"And more fun too," I said dropping my shorts.

"Do me first," I said.

He spread a towel on the bed and I lay down on it. He trimmed around the edges of my bush and down along the sides of my dick. Then he took a comb and combed through it and trimmed off the longer hairs. He picked up my dick and handed it to me.

"Here hold this out of the way," he said.

"It has a name," I said.

He stopped and grinned.

"And what would that be?"

"The Kraken."

He nearly fell over laughing.

"Well then hold The Kraken up out of the way."

I held my dick and he shaved my balls and down my crack. I lifted up my legs and he shaved my asshole. Then he took his hand and wiped away all the hair.

"Looks good," he said.

He took my dick from me and kissed the tip.

"Nice Kraken," he said.

He lay down and I started on his bush. His was thicker than mine and there was more of it. I shaped it nicely and then trimmed it down so it was shorter and more compact. Then he lifted up his dick and I shaved the sides and his balls.

"Does yours have a name?" I asked grinning.

"Yes, I call it Mucho Grande," he said.

We laughed like a couple of twelve-year old girls.

Then he lifted up his legs and I shaved his crack and butt hole. I brushed the hair away and licked across his butt hole.

"Oh yeah," he said.

"Get up."

He got up and we took the towel off the bed. We stood there and pulled on each other's cocks until we were both hard and then we lay down head to toe and sucked each other. Damn I loved his cock in my mouth.

We licked each other's balls and assholes and soon we were close to cumming.

"Evan, will you do something special for me?"

"Anything."

"I want to suck your toes and cum on your feet."

"Huh?" he said grinning.

"It's a thing I've got for feet."

"Kinky... I like it."

I took his feet in my hands and licked his soles and then licked and sucked his beautiful feet. They were as pretty as any I'd ever seen. He lay there watching me and reached up and took my cock in his hand and jacked me. I got the feeling and took my cock and jacked it onto his feet. I shot cum all over them. When I'd stopped dripping I lifted them up and licked my cum off each of them.

He looked up at me.

"That was pretty damn hot," he said.

"It was something I've wanted to do for a long time," I said.

"Well I've got something I've seen on videos but never tried."

"What?" I said grinning at him.

"A golden shower."

"You mean someone pissing on you?"

He nodded.

"You ever done it?"

He shook his head.

"I've watched it on videos and it made me so fucking hard, I kind of want to try it."

"My aren't we the kinky little Mexican?" I said.

"Si."

"Let's go to the shower," I said.

We went into his bathroom and he sat on the floor of the shower. I got in and closed the door.

"So I just piss on you?"

He nodded.

I took my cock in my hand and began pissing. I shot it on his chest and he moved forward and it went on his face. Then I got a surprise when he opened his mouth and let my piss run into it. I filled his mouth and the spit it out and I filled it again. By now I was out of piss and getting a hard-on. He leaned up and sucked my cock and jacked himself. A few minutes later I was ready to cum.

"Shoot it on my face," he said.

He began cumming and shot it up on his chest and belly and I came all over his face. When we were done he was covered with piss and cum.

"Freaky," I said. "How was it?"

"Pretty cool. Not something I'd do every day. But I liked it."

"Well if you want a kiss you're gonna have to shower," I said.

I held my hand down and pulled him up. He grabbed me and pulled me to him getting cum and piss all over my belly. Then he looked me in the eye and kissed me. I didn't give a shit about the piss and cum after all.

Joey called me and told me we had an appointment with our prospective landlord in four days

"Can you guys get off work to come and look at the place?"

"Evan's the assistant manager. It shouldn't be a problem."

"Let's plan on staying in the apartment Friday night and Saturday and having a celebration," Joey suggested. "After all Evan's over 21."

"He's 22."

"Cool then we can get some beers and mess around."

"Always thinking Joey," I said.

"That's why you love me," he said.

I told him I'd let him know by email. I told Evan and he was all for it.

"I think Joey might want to mess around," I said.

"You've messed with them before haven't you?"

"Yeah but that was before I met you. Now it's different."

"I understand. If it was okay with me would you like to do it?"

I grinned.

"They're both cute as hell and very horny."

"I'm not against it except I would rather keep making love to just you and me."

"I'm all for that. That's something special that I want only you and me to share."

"That's why I love you," he said and he kissed me.

We met the guys at a Wendy's four days later. I introduced Evan to Todd and Joey and they were like a couple of horny goats.

"Jakey, you did good," Todd said.

"Is he as good in bed as he looks?" Joey asked.

"Better," I said.

Evan blushed.

We met the landlord and looked at the place. It was nothing special but it had a decent kitchen, small living room, two bedrooms and a bathroom. We talked it over and signed a lease for the upcoming school year. We could move in whenever we liked.

He also took us to the back yard, which was very small but had a charcoal grill and a picnic table. The yard next door was fenced in and there were some huge piles of shit lying on the ground.

"What the hell kind of animal do they keep in that pen?" Joey asked.

"A dog," the landlord said.

"Holy crap it must be a huge dog. That shit looks like it came from an elephant."

The landlord laughed.

"Brutus is a very big dog. He's a St. Bernard."

"The brandy dog?" Joey asked.

"The very same. But Brutus has no brandy."

"Well, I hope he's friendly," I said.

"Oh he's a huge teddy bear."

After the landlord left we were pretty excited. Since Joey and Todd had found the place we let them pick which bedroom they wanted. The queen-sized beds and mattresses were there but that was all. We'd brought a couple of pillows and a blanket with us.

"Okay, first order of business, let's go and get some groceries and some adult beverages."

"You boys aren't old enough to drink," Evan said.

"Who you callin boy's Willis" Joey said.

"Let's go," Evan said laughing.

We went to a supermarket and got some frozen pizzas, chips, a box of Captain Crunch and a carton of milk. We got a big package of brats and hot dogs and some buns too for Saturday night. Joey was pushing the cart and when we went down the aisle with feminine products, Todd slipped a package of Kotex into the cart. We added three twelve packs of beer and went to the checkout.

Joey was clowning around while we put the stuff on the belt. We'd all chipped in a twenty-dollar bill and he was the banker. When the lady picked up the Kotex she looked at him and he nearly pissed his pants.

"You fuckers!"

"Joey, watch your mouth," I said.

"Oops sorry," he said.

The lady laughed.

"Every year we have that joke a dozen times when guys your age move into housing. She tossed the Kotex into a box under the counter that had three other packs in it.

"Good joke," Joey said. "Real original."

We went back to our place and put things away and then decided to cook the pizzas and relax with a fermented malt beverage.

The pizzas were gone and two of the twelve packs of beer were also gone and we were all getting a little goofy.

"Let's play something," Joey said.

"Like what?" Todd asked.

"Like something where we get naked," Joey said nodding his head up and down.

"We've only got on shorts, boxers and tee shirts. It won't take long for us to get naked," I said.

"Well then if you're naked the person who wins can tell you something to do."

"How do you win?"

"Don't make this complicated," Todd said.

"Sorry. How about we just all pull a card out of the deck and whoever has the lowest card loses?"

"Did you bring cards?" I asked.

"Well no."

I turned to Evan.

"You'd never know these guys were college students would you?"

"Fuck you Jake. If you're so smart you think of a game."

I looked around. There wasn't much to work with. I thought for a minute and then said, "Take off your boxers. Well put them in an empty beer box and each guy draws a pair one at a time and the person's boxers they draw has to do what he says."

"I like that," Evan said, "Simple and to the point."

"But no fucking," Evan said.

"We want to keep that something special between us," I said.

"That's understandable," Joey said.

We all dropped our shorts and took off our boxers. Todd and Joey were very impressed with Evan's big brown cock.

"Holy Toledo," Todd said. "Looks like a giant Tootsie Roll."

We all laughed.

"It doesn't have perforations in it."

"I'll do that with my teeth," Joey said.

We took off our shirts too because the game was going to get out of hand real quickly and we knew it.

"You first," I said to Joey.

He reached in the box and pulled out my boxers.

"Okay Jakey, let's see…"

He lifted up his cock and wagged it at me.

"Slurp on my sweet treat."

Like I didn't know that was going to happen.

I knelt in front of him and put his soft cock in my mouth and began sucking on it. Everyone suddenly had their cocks in hand and slowly jacked them as I sucked Joey. His cock began to grow. When it was fully hard I took it out.

"That's it," I said.

"No way. You have to suck me off."

"You didn't say suck you off, you said suck you and I sucked you."

"Well shit the bed. Oh wait, that was just an expression."

Evan was next. He drew Joey's boxers.

"He grinned at me and said to Joey, "Lick my balls."

Joey grinned and dropped to his knees. He lifted up Evan's cock and licked the underside of it and then began licking his balls. He sucked each one into his mouth and Evan jumped.

"Okay that's enough," I said. "Todd you're next."

Todd pulled his own boxers out.

"That's no good," he said. "I'm not doing something to myself."

He put them back and got Evan's.

"Bring that big chocolate cock over here and let me suck it… until you cum."

"That's not fair," Joey said.

"Fuck you Joey, you gotta be smart when you say your request."

Evan walked in front of Todd and he took his big cock in his hand and put his mouth over the head. I felt a little jealous watching him sucking my boyfriend but we'd agreed on it so I didn't say anything.

Todd sucked and jacked Evan for ten minutes and suddenly he gasped and I could tell Evan was cumming in his mouth. Evan shut his eyes and grunted several times.

Todd slurped on it and then took it from his mouth. He opened his mouth to show us a mouthful of cum. Then he swallowed it.

"Damn that was good," he said wiping his chin.

We went back and forth for an hour sucking and licking balls and assholes until everyone had cum at least twice. We were pretty tired out so we went to our bedrooms and said goodnight.

We put a blanket on the bed and a second one to cover us. I shut off the light and Evan and I got into bed naked and cuddled.

"I hope those guys didn't freak you out," I said hugging him.

"No I expected it. They're good guys. I think we're going to have a hell of a lot of fun here this next year."

We kissed and fondled and suddenly I heard Evan snoring lightly. I kissed his lips one last time and lay my head against his shoulder and slept… in my lover's arms.

The next morning we were sitting at the kitchen table eating Captain Crunch when we heard a sound coming from outside.

"Woooo woooo woooo."

"What the hell is that? Evan asked.

Todd looked out the window.

"I think that might be our neighbor Brutus," he said.

We all got up and looked and holy shit, the biggest dog I'd ever seen was standing with his face against the fence looking at us.

"Damn get a saddle and we can give pony rides," Joey said.

We walked out and there stood Brutus. His big tail was swishing back and forth. He must have stood over three feet tall at the shoulder. His head was the size of a basketball and he was slobbering all over the fence.

"Holy smokes, I've never seen a dog that big," Evan said.

"He's very friendly," a voice said.

We looked toward the house and there was a lady coming out of the door.

"He gets a lot of attention from the students who rent this place," she said gesturing to our new home. "They treat him and take him for walks so he thinks you guys are his new best friends."

"How much does he weigh?" I asked.

"He's pushing two hundred pounds. But he's as gentle as a kitten. His biggest problem is that he slobbers like a fountain."

Boy she was right. Slobber was dripping off him.

"He usually gets breakfast about now and I suppose he thinks you're going to feed him. The slobber gets worse when he's expecting food.

"I'll get him some cereal," Todd said running for the kitchen.

He came back a few minutes later with a mixing bowl with the last of our Captain Crunch in it and opened the gate. Brutus came lumbering out and plunged his face into the bowl and made a hell of a lot of crunching and slurping and in no time the cereal was gone. He then went to each of us and leaned up against us.

"He's saying hello," the lady said.

"So it's okay if we feed him and take him for walks and stuff?" Joey said.

"Just don't give him any beer or beans. You have no idea what a St. Bernard fart is like. He'll walk along with you but watch so he stays out of the street. I'd hate for a car to hit him and someone get hurt."

"It better be a big car or he'd wreck it," Todd said.

We spent the day making our little home our own. For lunch we went out for pizza but at dinnertime we made brats and hot dogs on the grill. Brutus stood by the fence making his "wooo" sound so we let him join us. He ate hot dogs like they were M & Ms.

After we'd eaten we sat in the back yard and talked and laughed until it got dark

"We need some more beer," Todd said.

"Evan and I will go get some," I said. "We'll take Brutus along."

We put a leash on the big mutt and he walked along swinging his tail as happy as a dog with fifteen hot dogs in his belly could be. There was a little corner grocery down the street. We got to the store and Evan looked at me and said, "We better leave him out here."

"Brutus, stay," I said.

He sat down in front of the door.

"Damn he's pretty smart," Evan said.

We went in and got a 24 pack of beer and while we were paying for it the clerk looked at the glass door and then looked at us with a kind of pissed off look.

"It that your mutt?"

"He's the neighbor's dog but he's with us."

"Well next time bring a squeegee."

We looked and Brutus had his nose against the glass door and there was about a quart of drool running down the door.

"Oh shit sorry," we said and hurried out.

Brutus walked with back to his house and we put him in his yard. He seemed happy.

We walked into our house and when we walked into the living room there was Todd on his back with his legs up in the air on either side of Joey. They were both naked and Joey was fucking the hell out of Todd. His ass was going like a bunny in a briar patch.

He looked up and grinned.

"Open me a beer huh?"

Evan looked at me.

"What have you gotten me into?"

The next few weeks Evan and I worked every available shift. We wanted to put away as much money as we could for our school year and our apartment. Of course our parents were paying the tuition and paying for our rent but we needed money for stuff like entertainment and beer.

I was counting the days until the love of my life and I could move in and start sharing our lives and our bed. It was hard at work to keep our hands off each other and whenever we got the chance we'd slip behind a door or into the cooler and have a few sweet kisses.

My mom invited Evan and his family for Lasagna night and we made sure not to have to worry about Evan's mom bringing some inedible dish by asking her to bring garlic bread. What could go wrong with that?

We had the dinner at Evan's out by their new pool. Evan and I were swimming when everyone got there so we just got out and dried off and joined the rest of them at the table.

There was a lot of talk of us leaving in two days for school. My mom and Evan's mom were gathering stuff for our kitchen and bathroom in the apartment.

"Honey what color sheets do you boys want for your beds?" Mom asked.

I looked at Evan. We hadn't told them there was only one bed.

"Well, um, I don't think we care about the color. But we only need sheets for one bed," I said.

"But aren't they twin beds? Or are they bunk beds?"

"Neither Mom. It's just one bed. One queen size bed."

My dad looked confused.

"We thought there would be beds like in a dorm."

Evan looked at me and I knew what he was thinking. It was time to tell them.

"Mom, Dad," he said, "Jake and I are more than friends. We didn't plan for it to happen but once we met we found we were attracted to each other and it's turned out that we love each other."

"Of course you do Honey, it's natural for best friends to love each other like brothers," his mom said.

"It's not like that," I said.

"Then what is it like?" Evan's dad asked. I could tell he already knew.

"Dad, Jake and I love each other like boyfriends... like lovers."

There wasn't a sound. All four of the parents sat there looking at us and Evan reached over and took my hand in his.

"You mean?" My dad said.

"Yeah Dad, Evan and I are in love like a guy and a girl would be. We love each other and have... sex with each other."

I felt like I was going to throw up.

Evan gripped my hand so tight my knuckle cracked.

The two moms looked at each other.

"Well then," his mom said, "do you have any preference in the color of the sheets for your one bed?"

"Um, I think blue would be nice," Evan said.

My mom got up and hugged me. Then she hugged Evan.

"If this is what life is going to be for my Jacob, then I'm glad it's with a fine young man like you."

Evan's eyes filled with tears.

The dads looked at each other and mine shrugged.

"Look," he said. "I'm not happy and I don't think any of us is happy about this but it's not the end of the world. Sure we're surprised. We've spent the last many years expecting daughters-in-law and grandchildren but if you two are happy, then I think we should be happy for you."

I felt like a car had been lifted off my chest.

"You guys can't believe how much that means to us. We've been trying to figure out what to do about telling you. We didn't want to keep lying to you, so this makes us very happy."

Evan put his arm around me and we hugged.

"Eat your lasagna, it's getting cold," my mom said.

Everyone began eating. I reached across and grabbed two pieces of garlic bread and gave one to the most beautiful boy in the world. We both took a bite and almost spit.

It was terrible. Instead of butter and garlic powder his mom had put some other spice on the bread and it tasted like fish.

"Mom what's that spice," Evan said putting the bread aside.

"Oh I thought I'd make it special and I put my Cod Surprise spices on it…do you like it?"

We're all moved in now and we've settled into our new lives. Todd and Joey are the best roommates we could ever find. They are such fun and so spontaneous that we just laugh and have fun all the time. You have to keep your guard up at all times or one of them will spring naked on top of you while you're studying or even sitting on the toilet. Brutus is our fifth roommate. As soon as one of us gets home from class we get him from his yard and he comes to our apartment and spends time with us. The big lug is just like a two hundred pound puppy. He nearly eats us out of house and home.

We have a lot of fun but we make sure we're all studying hard too. With the four of us there is always someone who understands something if someone else doesn't get it. Evan is brilliant. I found out that he had a straight 4.0 grade point in California. So I think we'll all do pretty well with our grades.

Evan and I took Brutus home and when we got back Todd and Joey were gone to bed. We could hear them in there laughing and I knew they were doing some strange position sexually. They came up with the wildest things.

We brushed our teeth and stripped down naked. We'd gotten used to sleeping naked since we usually ended up that way. I got in bed and Evan got in and lay on top of me and we began making out. Our cocks started getting hard right away. He was grinding into me as we kissed.

"Do you know how much I love you?" he asked.

"Tell me."

"I love you more than all of the drops of water in the ocean."

"Do you know how much I love you?" I asked.

"Tell me."

"I love you more than all the grains of sand in the desert."

"You're the guy I've always dreamed of Jake."

"You're my California Dream Boy."

And then Evan made love to me.

The Perfect Boy

I have lusted for Brandon Mathews for years. We met when we were freshmen in high school. We'd been in different middle schools and found ourselves thrown together with a lot of new kids when we entered high school.

I had no idea who he was but I knew he was one of the most beautiful boys I'd ever seen. He stood out among the rest of us boys. At age 13 or 14 most of us were gangly, uncoordinated and somewhat geeks. Brandon was perfect. He was tall, coordinated, unblemished and gorgeous.

I found during our high school years that he not only was a beautiful person physically, but he also was a beautiful person when it came to treating others with respect and friendship.

Brandon was one of those kids who smiled and talked to everyone in the halls and classes. It didn't matter if a girl was heavy or skinny, Brandon would talk to them just like he talked to the pretty cheerleaders.

Brandon entered high school nearly 6 feet tall and grew a couple of inches his freshman year. Of course he was a star basketball player, an ace pitcher on the baseball team, Prom king, class president, and a member of the honor society. But it never went to his head. Brandon could make even the biggest geek or the worst kid in the phys. Ed class feel good about themselves.

He and I were friendly in high school but never big pals. We always said hi and even worked together in a class project.

All the while I was in high school I watched him secretly and dreamed about him sexually. I've known I like boys since I was about 12 and Brandon was what every gay boy dreamed of.

The best word for him is perfect. He's tall, with a perfect body. He's not a big muscle head but has long powerful arms, a well-defined chest, flat stomach and gorgeous legs. Of course he's blond and his hair is naturally curly. He's worn his hair fairly long all the years I've known him and the loose curly circle his face making him almost too pretty to be a boy. He has pale blue eyes and a prefect smile.

I've always loved looking at his hands and feet. They are like works of art. His hands are smooth and he has long sensual fingers. His feet are perfect, with nicely shaped toes and he always keeps them looking wonderful.

He was Valedictorian of our class with a 3.98 GPA. He got a B in one class one semester.

And if all of that wasn't enough, his parents are both doctors and they have a butt load of money.

But Brandon never put on airs. He drove a used mini-van that he bought with money he earned during the summer and he never let on that he had ten times as much as the rest of us did.

My world changed when I went to the University and found Brandon in three of my classes the first year. I found out that he was Pre-Med and it turned out that I was Pre-Veterinary so we had a lot of science classes together. We teamed up in our labs as partners and soon became good friends.

Brandon never knew how much I desired him and I never had the guts to make any advances. I knew it was useless because he dated a lot of girls and often had two or three girls with him.

Brandon and I are both finished with our 3 years of study before moving on to a medical school and a veterinary school and are working at the same Taco Bell this summer. I'd applied for a job and been hired when he mentioned to me that he was looking for a job too. I told him about he Taco Bell job and he got in too.

We spent the weekend working and had the following Monday off and Brandon invited me over to show me a new game he'd bought for his Play-station. I'd never been to his house and was excited about seeing his room and where he lived.

When I got to the address I understood just how well off his parents were. They lived in a huge old Victorian house in a neighborhood of huge beautiful houses. Brandon met me at the door and I followed him upstairs to his room.

He was wearing an old tee shirt with the sleeves cut off and the bottom half cut off. His gorgeous belly was showing and so was his blond treasure trail that went into the top of an old pair of gym shorts. I drooled at the tufts of blond hair sticking out under his arms and took a good look at his beautiful feet, as he was barefoot.

I followed him up the stairs and could see his butt cheeks plainly under the thin cloth of the shorts. It was obvious he wasn't wearing underwear.

I had a semi-boner by the time we got upstairs and Brandon showed me his room. I'd watched his gorgeous butt and perfect legs as we climbed the stairs. He had a small amount of blond hair on his lower legs and the upper part was smooth and lovely.

"Well this is it," he said showing me the room.

Holy shit his room was bigger than my living room, kitchen and dining room put together. The first thing I noticed was a queen sized bed, which was made perfectly. There was a large walk-in closet full of clothes on hangers and on shelves, a big screen TV, a stereo and a big fish tank full of beautiful fish.

"Wow, you've got a huge room," I said.

"Yeah, it's really more than I need but my folks wanted me to have plenty of space," he said apologetically.

"Shit, I'd love to have something like this. My room is not as clean and orderly as this. Do you have a maid who cleans up?"

"No, I just try to keep it clean," he said.

Of course he did.

In front of the 60 inch flat screen there was a double recliner. Brandon offered me a seat and we sat and he turned on the Playstation. There was a consol between the two reclining seats that was refrigerated and full of sodas. I thought to myself, "this guy has it made."

We began playing and really had a good time. Not only was the game a lot of fun, it was great being so close to Brandon and looking at his legs and feet. I could smell his shampoo and the soap from his shower. I had a partial boner the whole time.

After a while Brandon asked me if I was hungry and I said I could eat. He went downstairs to get some snacks and I got up and looked around his room. He had a lot of nice stuff. In the back of the room there were big glass double doors and I walked over to them and saw that there was a small porch outside them. I opened the doors and walked out. There was a small table and a couple of deck chairs and a lounge chair that was lying flat like he'd slept on it. I imagined him lying there on a hot summer night in the nude and began boning up.

Just then I heard someone giggling and looked out toward the yard. Brandon's family had a nice pool and what looked like an outdoor kitchen in the fenced-in back yard. The pool was very blue and looked inviting. The grill and picnic area was very nice, with an outdoor refrigerator and what looked like all the things needed to make meals out there in the nice weather.

I heard the laughter again and looked to the neighbor's yard, which was just across the other side of the fence. They must have had money too because their yard had a pool and outdoor kitchen area too. What caught my eye were two teenage boys who were in the pool.

One was blond and pretty skinny. His long blond hair hung down in bangs on his face and covered his ears and hung down his back. I couldn't see much of his body because he was in the water but I could tell he was wearing a very skimpy red swimsuit.

The other by was very dark skinned. He had black curly hair that was fairly long and covered his ears. His skin was the color of milk chocolate. He was also wearing a skimpy swimming suit that looked to be bright yellow.

They both looked damn cute and I watched them farting around in the water, splashing each other and grab-assing each other. I heard Brandon come back into the room and was turning to go see what he'd brought to eat when I heard a yell. I turned back and the two boys were out on the pool deck. The blond kid had pulled the dark kid's suit down and was pulling it off his feet.

The dark kid was laughing and when his suit was completely off he reached up and pulled the blond kid's suit off. The blond kid had a nice boner which I could plainly see standing up from his dark blond pubes.

Then I really got freaked out. The dark kid knelt up and put the blond kid's cock in his mouth and began sucking him.

"Holy shit!" I said.

Brandon heard me and walked toward the balcony.

"What's wrong?" he asked.

I nodded toward the pool in the other yard. By now the blond kid had his hands on either side of the dark kid's head and was face-fucking him.

"Oh my God," Brandon said.

I turned to him.

"You know those kids?" I asked.

"The blond one lives next door, his name is Teddy. I think the other one is an exchange student. I've seen him over there before."

"Doing that?" I asked.

"Hell no. I never saw anyone doing that before."

Brandon was watching very closely and I noticed he adjusted his cock in his gym shorts.

Just then the dark kid got up and the two boys embraced and began kissing. We watched them kiss for a few minutes and then they ran holding hands into the house.

Brandon looked at me with an amazed look on his face.

"Wow," he said.

I had an obvious boner and he looked down at it. I didn't try to hide it.

"His room is right across from mine," he said quietly.'

I followed him into the room and we walked to the window that looked across to the other house. My mouth dropped open when we looked out.

The dark kid was lying on his back on the end of the bed and the blond kid has his cock up the other kids ass and was fucking the hell out of him. The dark kid's ass was a couple shades lighter color than his back and legs and it was as cute as hell. He had tiny feet typical for Mexican kids and they were adorable. His little toes were cute as hell and the bottoms of his feet were pinkish in contrast to the dark brown of the tops. He had his legs wrapped around the waist of the blond kid.

The blond kid was fucking like a damn bunny, his ass going full speed.

I noticed Brandon adjust his cock again as we watched. I began to wonder.

It didn't take long and the blond kid pulled his cock out of the other boy's ass and the other kid leaned up and took a load of cum right in the face. The blond kid squirted several jets of cum onto the other kid's cute face and he lapped it right up. Then the blond kid knelt down and the dark kid stood up and jacked his cock a few times and shot cum all over the blond kid's face.

"Fuck me," Brandon said to himself.

"No shit," I said.

We stood there mesmerized as the two kids embraced and began kissing again. Soon they walked hand-in-hand to what I supposed was the bathroom.

Brandon looked at me. "I'll be damned."

I grinned. "You never knew?"

"Hell no, Teddy's been my neighbor for years but I had no idea he was... was doing that. Don't you remember him?"

"No I don't think I know him.

"He was a freshman when we were seniors. He's a senior this year. We've been neighbors for a long time. His parents are friends of my parents. So we've had a lot of cookouts and stuff over the years. He just had his 18th birthday."

"Well, it looks like he's found a friend," I said.

"No shit," Brandon replied.

A few minutes later the boys came out of the bathroom with towels wrapped around their waists. They picked up the controllers for the kid's Play-station and sat down in a couple of chairs and began playing.

"Well the show is over," I said.

Brandon nodded.

We went back to this double recliner unit and he offered me chips and cheese and crackers and a soda.

I didn't know what to say so I just sat and ate.

"What did you think of that?" Brandon asked.

"Those guys having sex?" I said.

He nodded.

"I think they had a hell of a good time. Personally I thought it was really hot."

He looked at me.

"Have you ever?"

Oh boy. I didn't know what to say. If I lied and said it was gross I was a damn liar. If I told him I thought it was cool and did the same thing when I got the chance he might kick my ass out of the house and we'd never be friends again.

"I've screwed around a few times," I said.

"No shit?"

I nodded.

He thought for a minute, digesting that.

"So do you mind if I ask… are you gay?"

"Yeah Brandon, I am. Do you ever remember me dating a lot of girls? I realized I liked boys at about 8th grade. I never broadcasted it. No one knows but you and a few guys who I've fucked around with."

"Who?"

I smiled at him. "I can't say. You understand."

He nodded.

There was a long silence. Shit, I probably just fucked my friendship with this beautiful guy.

"Do you want me to go?" I asked.

"No," he said.

It was kind of uncomfortable sitting there and not talking. Finally Brandon turned and looked at me. Damn he was beautiful.

"I think you noticed I got a boner when we were watching those kids," he said.

"That's natural, even for a straight guy," I said.

"It might be, but I'm not sure I'm straight."

I felt like I'd been run over by a bus.

"What do you mean? You've dated dozens of girls, maybe hundreds of them."

He smiled. "Do you remember me ever having a girlfriend? Did you ever see me with just one girl?"

"Well, I guess not," I said.

"If I'd had one girlfriend or gone out with one girl I'd have had to "perform". I mean I'd have had to have sex with her. But with a bunch of them I could just laugh it off. I got all the girls I wanted because I'm fairly good looking and have money. Girls go for that shit."

My mind was reeling.

"Wait, so you're telling me you've never had sex with a girl?"

He nodded.

"Oh my God. Have you had sex with a guy?"

He smiled at me. "Not yet."

I thought I was having a stroke. My head hurt and my ears were ringing.

"You're a virgin at 21?"

He nodded.

"Unless you count jacking off. I've done that about 15,000 times since I was 12."

I laughed at him.

"Brandon you're probably the best looking boy who ever graduated that school and you've spent 3 years in college and never had sex with another person. Am I getting that correct?"

He nodded. "I didn't want sex with a girl and I was afraid to do something with a guy for the fear that my parents would find out. They expect a lot from me. They're both successful doctors, I'm the golden child. They expected me to be prefect and get perfect grades and I suppose marry a perfect girl and raise a batch of perfect grandkids for them. But I think they're going to be disappointed. It'll probably kill them. They just about had a heart attack when I got that one B in high school. I can't imagine what telling them I'm gay would do."

I didn't know what to say. How many times had I wished I was as good-looking as him or had as much money or was as smart as he was? Then I find out it wasn't so great after all?

"Wow, that's a lot to digest," I said.

He smiled his perfect smile and put his perfect hand on my arm.

"I know it is. It's very hard for me to say all of this but I feel I can trust you. I've watched you for a long time and I always thought that you might be gay. It wasn't that you did anything obvious but I noticed you looking at me now and then and just had a notion.

"You got me," I said grinning.

"So… what do you think?" he asked.

"What do I think about what?"

"What do you think about teaching me about man to man love?"

My heart was beating so fast I thought I was going to pass out. Did I hear right? Did Brandon Mathews just ask me to teach him about gay sex? Are you fucking me?

"Ricky, what do you think?" he said.

Brandon is the only person who calls me Ricky. My name is Richard and that's what my parents call me. Many of my friends call me Dick and a few call me Rick but Brandon has always called me Ricky.

"Brandon you're not just fucking with me are you? I mean you're serious?"

He nodded. "I've been wanting this for a long time. I don't want to have some anonymous sex in a restroom or an alley. I want to learn with someone I care about."

Brandon cares about me? Wow!

"Brandon, I'd love to teach you. To be honest I've lusted for you since the first time I saw you the first day of 9th grade. I thought you were the most beautiful boy I'd ever seen and now, all these years later you're even more beautiful."

"You think I'm beautiful?"

"Of course, there's nothing about you that isn't perfect," I said.

"I think you're beautiful too Ricky. I've always thought you were so cute and now so handsome. I've had you in my mind many times when I jacked off."

Gulp! Brandon Mathews thinks I'm beautiful? I've never thought of my self as beautiful but adequate. I'm a strong six feet tall, weigh about 160 and have a pretty good body. My hair is just a common light brown and I keep it kind of short and preppy. I've got nice blue eyes and a good smile. I'm pretty well fixed in the dick department. I've got about 6inches and my dick is real thick. I've messed with a fair number of guys and have seen a few dicks that are longer and a few shorter so I think I'm about average.

"So, what, what do you want to do?" I asked.

"I want to go slow and learn. I want us to act like lovers not like sex in a back alley."

"Brandon I've loved you for years, that won't be hard," I said.

I stood up and motioned for him to do the same. He stood up and I could see his cock standing up toward his belly. It was hard and looked damn big. He looked down at mine, which was sticking straight out and making a wet spot on the front of my shorts.

I stepped toward him and put my arms around him. He kept his eyes right on mine and I leaned forward and kissed him on the lips. He moaned.

He put his arms around me and pulled me tightly to him. I could feel his boner pushing against mine. He began kissing me and soon our tongues were dueling in each other's mouth.

I thought I was dreaming. I opened my eyes and looked at the face I'd dreamed about for 7 years and that face was Brandon's and he was kissing me. Wow!

Soon I ran my hands down his back, feeling the muscles and making him moan with delight. He began rubbing my back too and I pushed into him so our cocks were mashing together.

"Oh man," he said.

I put my hands on his gorgeous ass and felt his ass cheeks. His tongue was in my mouth and probing deeply. I squeezed his ass cheeks and he humped into me and began to groan.

"Oh no!" he said.

I felt something wet on my dick and looked down. Brandon had cum in his shorts.

His cock was throbbing and a big wet spot was growing in the fabric.

"Oh Ricky I'm so sorry," he said with tears in his eyes.

"Brandon, hey, it's okay."

"But I spoiled the moment," he said.

I kissed his cheeks and tasted his tears.

"Brandon, it's okay. We can stop here or we can wait a while and try again, it's alright with me either way."

"You haven't cum," he said.

"I can do that any time. Don't worry," I said.

His face was all flushed. "I feel like such a fool."

I laughed. "Brandon I've had a few pre-event ejaculations myself. Sometimes you just can't help it. Let's go and take a shower and get you cleaned up and try again."

He smiled and led me to his bathroom. I stood back and watched him as he took his clothes off. First he pulled his tee shirt over his head and there was his perfect body. His armpits were filled with thick blond hair. His nipples were very light colored and about the size of a dime. He was beautifully built. Then he pulled his shorts down and I caught my breath. His cock was wet and had cum on it and it was just as beautiful as I'd imagined it would be.

Brandon's pubic bush was just as blond as his hair on his head. It was trimmed, as I'd expected it to be. His cock hung down a good 4 inches and possibly a little longer. He was circumcised and his balls hung low in a nearly hairless sack below his cock head. He looked down at himself.

"Is it okay?"

"Brandon it's as perfect as any I've ever seen. It's beautiful," I said taking hold of it. He kind of jumped when I touched his cock.

"Show me," he said looking at my crotch.

I pulled my shirt off and kicked off my flip-flops. Then I dropped my shorts and stood there in all my glory. My cock was still fully hard and sticking straight out at him. My bush is light brown and full, my balls are good sized and hang nice and loose.

"It's fat," he said.

"I'll put it on a diet," I said.

He looked at me and realized I was fucking with him and he laughed.

"No I like it like it is," he said. Then he looked at me and said, "May I?"

I nodded and he took hold of my cock and milked it. A big drop of precum oozed out the slit. He looked at it and took his finger in it and wiped if off. He put his finger up to his mouth and licked it off.

"Oh," he said.

I reached over and took his cock in my hand. It was hard again and standing up at attention. I began playing with it and soon precum oozed out of the tip. I looked up at him.

"May I?"

He grinned and nodded. I knelt down and took his cock into my mouth. Brandon gasped and nearly tipped over backward.

I pulled down on his balls and his cock was right in my face. I took it as deep as I could go and had his pubes in my nose. His cock was close to 7inches and a perfect thickness.

"Oh man," he said when I took it deep.

I bobbed up and down on him and then I took his balls and licked them, sucking each one of them into my mouth. He had his head back and was barely breathing.

"Slow down or I'll cum again," he said.

"That's okay," I said.

"No I want to do you first," he said.

I let his beautiful cock loose and stood up. He knelt on the floor in front of me and took my cock in his hand like it was going to attack him. He leaned forward and licked the precum off the tip. Then he looked up and me and smiled and opened his mouth and took it about half way. He gagged a little but didn't quit. Soon he was taking more and more.

"Brandon you don't have to go all the way on it. It's a mouthful. Take your time," I said.

As excited as I was I knew this wasn't going to last very long. I wanted to try to cum together.

"Brandon let's lay on your bed and 69," I said.

He got up and almost ran to the bed. He lay down and I lay the other way and soon we were slurping on each other's cocks. He was really getting into it and was taking my cock almost to the pubes. I could get his down so my nose was buried in his balls.

"Oh I'm close," he said.

"Me too," I mumbled around a mouthful of cock.

"You don't have to take it in your mouth," I said.

"I want to."

I knew it was over in the next minute. My cock began to tickle and I began squirting cum into his mouth. He kind of jumped when the first shot hit him but he kept sucking. I was holding my breath as I came and suddenly cum shot out of Brandon's cock and down my throat. I wanted to taste it so I slipped my lips around his cock head and caught the rest in my lips. We both kept sucking until we were both soft.

We lay back on the bed and both of us were panting. I looked down at Brandon's face and he was flushed. He looked up and me and smiled and then he got up and switched ends. He lay with his gorgeous face inches from mine and he leaned over and kissed me.

"I've been waiting for that for a long time," he whispered.

"Was it what you expected?" I asked.

"It was. Thank you," he said.

My heart felt like it would burst. The most beautiful boy I'd ever known was thanking me for having sex with him. I kissed him deeply and wrapped my arms around his naked body.

"For as long as I live, I'll never forget this moment," I said.

We sat up and I looked across the room and there were the two kids from next door, kneeling at the blond kid's bedroom window... watching us.

"Uh oh," I said.

Brandon looked where I was looking and gasped.

"Oh fuck, they've been watching us."

I got up with my limp dick swinging and walked to Brandon's window. They ducked down. I opened the window and looked across between the two houses.

"Hey, we know you were watching," I said.

Two heads appeared from below the window.

"Sorry," the blond kid said.

"It's okay," I said, "we watched you fucking earlier."

The kid grinned. "Did you like it?"

I had to laugh. "Yeah you looked like a damn bunny, who's your friend?"

"This is Taco. His real name is Manuel but I call him Taco."

"*Hola,*" the kid said.

I grinned. Why don't you two come over here to the back yard and we'll talk."

"Is Brandon pissed?"

"No don't worry we're not going to do anything to you we just want to talk."

"Okay, we'll be over."

Brandon was standing behind me.

"What are you going to do?" he asked.

"I think we should talk to them and make it clear that we don't want them blabbing what they saw," I said.

"Good idea, my parents would freak," Brandon said.

"What, the golden boy likes dick and they can't tolerate it?"

He nodded. "Yeah something like that."

We put our shorts on and walked barefoot and shirtless to the back yard. The two kids had already come through the gate in the fence and were sitting on a couple of lawn chairs. They were wearing their speedos.

Teddy had a shit-eating grin on his face when we walked up to them.

"Fucking A Brandon," I didn't know you liked dick," he said.

"Yeah, well you learn something every day."

I looked Teddy and Taco over and they were cute as hell. Brandon had told me Teddy was 18 but Taco looked pretty young.

"Does he speak English?" I said to Teddy.

He laughed. "Taco, comprende English?"

Taco grinned, "Fucking A I speak English."

I laughed.

"How old are you Taco?" I said.

"I'm older than Teddy," he said in perfect English.

"You're an exchange student?"

"Yup."

"Teddy you sure as hell don't look 18," I said.

"I'm a late bloomer. I didn't get pubes until nearly my junior year in high school. I was too small to play basketball and football so I went out for soccer. Us little guys are good at running and kicking."

"You look cute in those little shorts too," I said.

Teddy grinned. "That too."

"So what's the story with Taco?"

"I came for a year here and the people I live with don't have any kids. They were happy when I made friends with American kids and when Teddy and I found out we both liked boys we became friends," he said.

"So you two are fucking regularly?"

They both grinned.

"Every chance we get," Teddy said.

Brandon stood there taking it all in.

"Teddy you gotta keep your mouth shut about this," he finally said.

"Hey, it's cool," Teddy said.

"You promise?"

"Hey, no problem, but um, Taco thinks it'd be fun to mess around with you guys… maybe like payment for us keeping quiet."

"You little fucker," Brandon said. "You mean like blackmail."

"No we'd just like to get a close-up look at those dicks of yours and play a little."

I looked at Brandon and grinned.

"I gotta think about that," he said.

"How about tomorrow? We'll come over and have a little pool party," Teddy said.

Brandon looked at me and I nodded.

"Okay tomorrow. We have to work at 4pm so we better do this in the morning."

"Taco is staying overnight."

"Okay," Brandon said.

The two little guys jumped up and I could see they both had boners. Taco's was standing up and the tip peaked out of his speedo. Teddy's was up over his left hip and looked damn big for such a little kid. Teddy reached out and took hold of Brandon's cock and pulled on it a little. He grinned.

"Fucking A," he said. They went to the gate and opened it.

"See you about 10," Teddy said. Then they both dropped their swimming suits and showed us their butts.

I shook my head.

"Well, what do you think?" I said to Brandon when they'd shut the gate.

"I don't know. I know I liked what we did and I want to do more, but I'm a little uneasy messing with those kids."

"They're legal age," I said, "and they probably know more about it than we do."

"Maybe we should practice," Brandon said.

"What?"

"My folks are at a seminar in Ohio. I'm home alone for the week. Why don't you stay over tonight and we'll have some lessons."

I grinned. "I could do that."

My dick was already hard as we walked into the house.

Brandon got a couple of T-bone steaks out of the freezer and put them in the microwave to defrost them. He was getting some potatoes ready to bake and I was making a salad for each of us. We were both still in just our shorts and it was very lovely working with this beautiful guy in the kitchen. I watched him as he worked, his tan skin looking so healthy, his beautiful hair circling his gorgeous face. I loved seeing the armpit hair when he raised his arm and the look of his perfect feet.

I began boning up.

Brandon was standing at the counter wrapping potatoes in foil and I walked up behind him and put my arms around his chest. He smiled and leaned back into me and turned his head. We kissed.

"I'm the luckiest guy in the world," I said in his ear.

"Why is that?"

"Because I've met the most beautiful man in the world and I've made love to him."

I pushed my crotch against his ass and he felt my hard dick against his ass crack.

"What's that?" he asked grinning.

"That's a treat for you when you're ready," I said.

He turned and put his arms around me and pulled me tightly against him. I could feel his hard cock against mine. He looked deeply at me with his pale blue eyes.

"I want to do it," he said.

"Now?"

He nodded. "This stuff will wait," he said. "The potatoes will take an hour to bake." Then taking me by the hand and leading me to the pool. There was a lounge that he laid down flat and then he embraced me again. My heart was hammering in my chest.

"Brandon, are you sure?" I asked.

"I'm sure," he said. "I've been thinking of this for years. I wanted to find the right guy to do it with and I've found him."

I had all I could do to keep from crying.

I put my hands on his shorts top and pulled them down. They dropped to the cement and he stepped out of them. I gasp looking at his beauty. From head to toe he was perfect. His dick was throbbing and leaking.

I pulled my shorts down and stepped out of them. He looked down at my hard cock and smiled.

"How do we do this?" he asked.

"We can go doggy style, face to face, or you can sit on my lap," I said.

"Face to face," he said.

I was all for that. I could watch his gorgeous face while we made love.

I bent down and sucked his cock for a minute and licked off the precum. Then I motioned for him to lie on his back on the lounge. He lay down and I lay on top of him and we began making out.

Brandon humped up into me and was sticking his tongue half way down my throat. I got on my knees and lifted his legs up. He took hold of them and pulled them up toward his chest. I looked down below his balls and there was his perfect asshole. It was pink and completely hairless. I put my finger against it and rubbed.

Brandon moaned.

I lubed up my finger and slid it into his ass. He shut his eyes and began groaning. After a minute I slid in a second finger. Then after another minute I put in a third finger.

"Oh man, oh man," he whispered.

"I gotta loosen you up," I explained.

He nodded that he understood.

"Okay, I'm going to put my dick in now... are you ready?"

"I'm as ready as I'll ever be," he whispered.

I lubed up the head of my cock with spit and put it up to his hole.

"Push back when I push and it will open up," I said.

I pushed my dick head against his pucker and he did as told and my dick head slid into his ass. He gasped and clenched at it with his ass muscle.

"I'll hold it until you're ready," I said.

He had his eyes closed.

"Do some more," he said.

I pushed and another inch went in. He grimaced but didn't say anything. I put in another inch and soon had all 6 inches in him. My pubes were against his ass and my balls were slapping against his butt cheeks.

"Are you okay?"

"It's very full feeling," he said.

"I can pull out," I said.

"Oh God no," he said looking at me. "Make love to me Ricky."

I began to fuck the most beautiful boy I'd ever known. I started slowly to let him get used to it and soon I picked up speed. Brandon began making a little "uh" noise every time I slid into him. We fucked like that for several minutes.

He had his hands on my ass and was pulling me into him trying to get more cock.

"Oh man, now it feels amazing. I never thought it would be so great feeling," he said.

I was glad he was enjoying it because I sure as hell was enjoying it.

Soon I felt my dick begin to get that feeling. I was hammering into him and I knew it wasn't far from the end for me.

"Brandon I'm about to cum," I said.

"Cum in me Ricky," he said looking up at me.

I slammed into him three more times and then held it all the way in while my cock squirted cum into this beautiful guys ass. I leaned forward and put my mouth on his and we kissed while I came inside him. He wrapped his arms around me and nearly crushed me.

Finally I stopped cumming and I lay on top of him panting. I could feel his heart beating against my chest. We both were sweating and panting. Brandon was rubbing my back and ass with his hands.

"Oh Ricky, oh fuck man, that was amazing," he whispered into my ear.

"I'm glad you liked it Brandon," I said. "I've jacked off to that picture in my mind a hundred times over the years."

He laughed. "Was it as good as you thought it would be?"

I looked at his beautiful face.

"Brandon if I died right this minute, I'd die the happiest guy in the world."

He pecked me on the lips.

"Well for God's sake don't die. How would I explain to my parents? Hey mom and dad, Ricky dropped dead by the pool after he fucked my brains out."

I laughed and hugged him. What a lucky fucker I was.

My dick was soft and slid from his ass. I looked down and his dick was hard as hell and leaking.

"Brandon lay back and let me do you," I said.

He grinned. "Ok," he said.

He lay back on the lounge and put his hands up over his head exposing his blond armpit hair. I knelt between his legs and took his cock and licked the shaft and up to the head. Then I sucked the precum out of the slit and took him into my mouth. I played with his big balls with one hand and held onto his cock with the other. I was going deeply on him and soon he began to shudder.

"Oh I'm close," he gasped.

I went as deep as I could and let his cock slip into my throat. I felt it throb and pulled back to his dick head was between my lips. Jet after jet of sweet cum shot out of his slit and I swallowed every drop. I sucked on his dick head like a sucker and soon he pushed my head away.

"Oh fuck, I can't take it any more. It's too sensitive," he gasped.

I licked his slit one more time and then sat back on my haunches.

"Well?" I said.

"Damn, damn, damn."

I laughed.

"I've been missing that for all of these years? I can't believe we didn't get together when we were in 9th grade. Just think of all the cum we could have made between then and now," he said grinning.

"We've got a long time to make cum together," I said.

I leaned down and we kissed.

"Ricky, I think I love you," he whispered into my ear.

"I KNOW I love you Brandon," I said.

I got off the lounge and we both stood up with limp dicks.

"Let's take a swim and cool off and then we can grill those steaks," he said.

We swam for a bit and then dried off. We went into the house and got the now baked potatoes, the steaks and the salads and a couple of bottles of beer. Brandon fired up the grill and, of course, cooked the steaks to perfection. We sat nude and ate our steaks and drank our beer. Damn, I felt like I was in a dream.

After we'd finished eating we cleaned up the mess and settled on Brandon's double recliner with another beer. We were still naked. For some reason we both felt very comfortable being naked together and I loved the idea of being with Brandon and being able to see every inch of him.

We talked about work and school. Brandon got us each another beer and then we decided to go to bed. He gave me a guest toothbrush and after we'd gotten ready for bed, we got into is queen sized bed naked.

Brandon lay on his back and I lay up next to him. He put his arm around me and we snuggled there. I could feel the heat from his body against mine. It was the most perfect feeling I'd had in years.

"I could get used to this," I said.

He looked at me and smiled his beautiful smile.

"This is nice. I've laid awake so many nights wishing I had someone to cuddle with, someone I could share my love with."

I didn't dare speak or I'd start to cry.

"Brandon, I'd like you to make love to me," I said quietly.

He looked at me.

"You mean?"

I nodded.

He smiled his 1,000watt smile.

"I'd like that," he said.

We began making out and soon both of us had raging boners. Brandon began humping into me and I knew he was ready.

"Do you want to do it the way we did?" he asked.

"I want to sit on it," I said.

He grinned. "I like that idea."

He rolled over on his back and we threw the blankets back. He looked magnificent lying there with his hands behind his head, his gorgeous body stretched out and his big thick cock standing up. I leaned down and sucked him for a couple of minutes.

"You better not do that much longer or I'll cum," he said.

I grinned. I lubed up his dick with some spit and then I straddled him. I guided his cock into my hole. I knew it was going to hurt. Brandon's cock head was a big one.

He closes his eyes as I pushed down on him.

Suddenly his cock head slid into my ass.

"Oh wait! Don't move," he said.

I knew what was happening. It had happened to me a few times too. The sudden grip of a guy's ass ring on a cock head made me cum several times and that was what was happening to him.

"Oh fuck, I almost came when it went in," he said grinning.

"Okay now?"

He nodded, so I began to work his big cock up my ass. Soon my cock was resting on his belly and my balls and his balls were crunched together.

"Oh man, it's tight," he said.

I smiled and began to work up and down on his cock. He took hold of mine and began to jack me. I reached down and pinched his nipples, which caused him to giggle. We were like a well-oiled machine. But it wasn't going to take that long because we were both very hot.

"I'm about there," he said.

"Let it shoot in my ass," I replied.

I impaled myself on his cock as deeply as I could go and felt him throb inside me. I knew his glorious cum was shooting into my ass and the thought made me shoot cum from my cock onto his chest and chin. He milked me dry and I lay forward on him panting.

We lay there just catching our breath. I felt his cock getting smaller and suddenly it slipped from my ass. I hated to feel it come out.

"How was that my gorgeous friend?" I asked.

"It was as good at I thought it would be and then ten times better," he said.

We kissed deeply.

We lay there for a little while longer and then got up and took a shower together. We each washed each other's hair and then soaped up each other's bodies and cocks and rinsed off. When we got out of the shower we dried each other off and walked hand-in-hand to the bed.

We lay down and Brandon pulled the quilt over us. I snuggled against him and he put his arms around me and kissed me.

"Good night my love," he whispered.

I tear ran down my cheek.

Sun streamed in the window and I woke confused. I didn't know for a few seconds where I was. Then I felt Bandon's body spooned up against mine and felt his strong arm across my chest.

Dang, I wasn't dreaming after all. I was in bed with the guy I'd dreamed about for years and we'd had sex three times yesterday.

Brandon stirred and I felt his boner against my ass. He leaned forward and kissed my cheek.

"Good morning Ricky," he said.

"Good morning gorgeous," I replied.

"Did you sleep well?"

"I slept great and waking up with a naked beautiful Brandon in my bed was even better."

He chuckled. "I like where my dick is right now too," he said as he poked me in the ass with his boner.

"Put it in," I said.

"What? Really?"

"Lube it and put it in," I said huskily.

Brandon lubed up his dick and I felt it in between my ass cheeks. He moved it up and down until he found my hole and then he gently shoved it in. I gasped a bit and he stopped.

"Don't stop, keep going," I said.

He began humping into me and soon he was fully inside me.

"Oh Ricky that feels amazing," he cooed into my ear.

"It's amazing for me too, my love," I said.

Brandon fucked me gently and after several minutes he pushed in as far as he could go and I felt his cock throbbing as he came in my ass. He let out a breath and I felt his cock slip from my ass.

"Oh man, what a way to wake up," he said.

I turned over on my back and looked up at him. He had a little sweat on his sweet face.

"That was lovely," I said.

He looked down at my hard cock.

"You need to cum," he said.

He took my cock in his mouth and began sucking me. He played with my balls and licked my shaft and in no time I was getting the feeling.

"I'm close," I said.

He took my cock as deep as he could get it and I unloaded in his throat. He sucked me dry and then leaned up and kissed me. I could taste cum on his tongue.

I pushed some hair out of his eyes and kissed him again.

"You're a perfect lover," I said.

"How's that?"

"Some guys just want to cum and then they're all done. You came and then made me have a great cum too. That's a perfect lover plus you're so damn beautiful."

"Did you call me your love?"

I thought back.

"Yes I did say that," I replied.

"Do you mean it?"

"Brandon I love you more than life itself."

Tears formed in his lovely blue eyes. He hugged me hard and I heard him gently sobbing.

"Brandon what's wrong? Did I say something wrong?"

"No, I'm just so happy. Everyone thinks I'm the lucky guy with looks and money and all of what everyone wants, but I always have been looking for just one thing to make my life complete. That's you Ricky. I love you."

Now it was time for both of us to cry.

We showered and managed to keep our hands off each other's dicks. Then we made breakfast and took it out to the pool to eat. We both each were wearing a pair Brandon's boxers. He and I wore the same size and the ones I had were from yesterday so he lent me a pair. I loved the idea of wearing his clothes.

Once we finished breakfast we lay back in a couple of lounge chairs and talked and just rested. It had been a pretty exciting previous 24 hours. I heard the latch on the gate and looked to see Teddy and Taco coming through, huge grins on their faces. They were wearing their speedos and it was apparent they both had boners. Taco's dick head was peeking up over the top of his suit and Teddy's boner was lying against his left hip.

"So, is it safe?" Teddy asked.

"What do you mean?" Brandon said.

"I mean are your parents gone to work?"

"They're out of town," Brandon said.

The two kids looked at each other and three seconds later they were both naked, their speedos lying on the skirt of the pool.

They were both cuties too. Taco's skin was a chocolate brown with a lighter area around his crotch where his speedo usually was. He had a nice black bush and his cock was uncut and standing right up against his belly button. It was medium thickness and about 5 inches long. His balls were nice sized and hung low. He had a cute face and beautiful dark eyes. His teeth were very white against his dark skin.

Teddy looked cute as hell too. He was also smallish built and thin. His little nipples were hard and he had a nice little tuft of blond hair under his arms. His eyes were bright blue and they went well with his longish blond hair. He had a hell of a cock for a kid as small as he was. It stuck up toward the left of his belly and looked to be close to 6 inches long. It was cut and nearly as thick as Brandon's.

I looked at their feet and they both had adorable small feet that were very cute.

"So you guys gonna get naked?" Teddy asked.

"What did you want to do?" I asked.

"Well we thought we'd both like to suck your cocks and then have you guys fuck us," he said matter-of-factly.

"Oh I see," I said grinning.

I looked at Brandon and he didn't look sure of it.

"So if we let you suck us and we fuck you that's it?" he asked.

"Yup, we'll never say a word and your secret is safe. If you feel like you need to suck us or do something else, we'd be happy to accommodate you for that too," he said.

"What do you think?" he asked me.

"I think it's okay. I'd like to tap one of those cute little asses anyway."

He grinned. "You want chocolate or vanilla?"

Taco stepped forward.

"Do me, I want that big fat cock of yours in my butt."

Teddy nodded.

"We already chose. I've been watching Brandon walk around in his room in his underwear and naked for years. I've probably jacked off ten gallons of cum watching him. I want to suck that cock and then get it in my ass."

"You've been watching me?"

"Fuck yeah. I've seen you jack off a lot of times. I did it with you too."

"Well I'll be."

I laughed. "There you go, time to give him a good fucking," I said.

Brandon and I stood up and took off our boxers. We both had boners and the two kids came for them. Taco dropped to his knees in front of me and took about ¾ of my dick into his throat. This kid knew how to suck a cock.

Teddy had hold of Brandon's cock and was licking it like a popsickle. He nuzzled Brandon's nuts and then took the head of his cock into his mouth and got damn near the whole thing down his throat. Brandon gasped when he did that.

"Holy fuck, you've done this a few times," he said.

"Fucking A."

We stood there with the boys sucking our dicks and then Brandon took a step my way and we were close enough to make out. We embraced and kissed while the boys sucked us.

I was getting pretty close so I told Taco to slow down.

"You keep doing that and I'll cum," I said.

"Oh no, I want that in my ass," he said.

He took my cock from his mouth and crawled up on the lounge. He knelt on all fours and I straddled the lounge and moved in behind him. I took hold of his cute little butt cheeks and pulled them apart. His little crack was lighter colored and had a few black hairs around his hole. I leaned in and licked his pucker hole and he moaned.

"Oh yeah, put that *magnifico* dick in me," he said.

I looked over and Brandon was lying on his back with Teddy squatting over his cock. Teddy held his balls up out of the way and had hold of Brandon's cock guiding it to his hole.

I put some spit on my dick head and pushed it into Taco's hole. I slipped in easier than I expected.

"Aye carumba!" he said.

Teddy was moaning as he lowered himself onto Brandon's cock. I looked at Brandon and he smiled at me.

I gave Taco the whole 6 fat inches of my cock and he took it like a man. The kid had been fucked before that was for sure. Soon my nuts were slapping against his and he was panting.

I reached around in front of him and took hold of his cock. The end was wet with precum. I began jacking him as I fucked him and soon I felt my cum getting ready to shoot.

"Are you close?" I asked.

"Very," he said.

I jacked him and slammed into is ass and my dick started squirting into his brown little butt. I felt his cock throb and knew he was shooting onto the lounge chair.

I looked over and Brandon was jacking Teddy furiously and just as I looked I saw cum shoot out of Teddy's cock and all over Brandon's chest. I saw Brandon close his eyes and knew he was cumming in Teddy's ass.

The fucking wound down and we all sat and caught our breath. I pulled my limp cock from Taco's ass and he lay over on his back.

"Extraordinaria," he panted.

Teddy was lying on Brandon's chest. His own chest was heaving.

"Fuck me, that was worth waiting for," he said.

"No disappointment?" Brandon asked.

"Fuck no. Damn that was hot. I'll jack off to that for years."

Brandon and I laughed. These were a couple of cute kids.

We were all sweating and covered with cum so we all trooped into the house to the master bath and got into the huge shower. It had one of those rain heads and we all soaped up and washed ourselves, and each other. By the time we were finished both Teddy and Taco had boner again.

We walked back out to the pool and the two kids stood there looking at each other's boner.

"What are we gonna do with these," Teddy asked.

"Is too bad we have no one to fuck," Taco said looking right at Brandon and me.

"Yes, that is a waste."

"What time is it?" I asked.

Teddy was wearing a watch.

"It's two thirty," he said.

"We've got time," I said to Brandon.

"We have to be at work at 4."

"Well, a quick fuck, another shower and we're off," I said.

Brandon grinned and knelt on the lounge.

"Let's go Teddy," he said.

I looked at Taco. "Back or front?"

"I would like very much to do you doggy style like Brandon and Teddy are doing," he said.

I knelt and Taco got behind me. He didn't waste any time. He pulled my ass cheeks apart and began licking my asshole. He lubed me up and the next thing I knew his cock was half way into my ass. It went in easy and was very pleasurable to be fucked with.

I looked over and Teddy was still licking Brandon's ass. He looked at me and grinned. "Fucking A."

He finally got up and bent his boner down so it would go into Brandon's ass. He went slowly and Brandon took it like a man. Soon both of the boys were fucking us like a couple of bunnies.

Teddy came first. I saw him close his eyes and he pushed all the way in and held it. He was cumming in Brandon's ass.

Then I felt Taco push all the way in and he held it. I felt his cock throbbing and knew he was cumming too.

They both held for a bit and then they pulled out semi-limp cocks.

"Holy shit, my life is complete," Teddy said.

"I can go back to Mexico and know I fucked a hot ass of a handsome American," Taco said smiling.

"Are you both satisfied?" I asked.

"Absolutely," Teddy said.

"*Gracias,*" Taco said. "I will remember this day for my whole life."

I leaned down and kissed the little shit and he hugged me. I kissed Teddy too and Brandon kissed both of them. They picked up their speedos and walked to the gate.

"Thanks, it was great," Teddy said.

They walked through and closed the gate.

I turned to Brandon. "Happy kids," I said.

"I liked it too," he said.

"You got that right."

We stopped at my house and I got my uniform for Taco Ball and some clothes. I told my mom I was staying at Brandon's since his parents were away.

We worked our shift and finished a little after midnight. When we got back to Brandon's house we stripped down and showered and then lay naked in his bed talking.

"Where are you going to live this semester?" he asked me.

"I haven't found a room yet. I figured to start looking for a place soon. Do you have a place?" I reached over and brushed some blond curls off Brandon's forehead.

"My folks leased an apartment for me. It's real close to the University. They've got a 5year lease on it. That way I can stay in one place until I finish Med. School."

"That's what comes from having wealthy parents. Mine can't afford something like that. But it's okay, I don't need anything fancy."

"Why don't you live with me?"

My heart skipped a beat.

"You mean it?"

He turned to me and embraced me and kissed me. "I think I'm in love with you Ricky. I'd like us to live together."

I had a hard time to speak.

"I know I love you Brandon, I'd love to live with you forever."

He held me tightly for a long time.

"The apartment is near the campus. I know the Veterinary School is close enough for you. It'd be perfect for both of us."

I couldn't keep from smiling.

"There's only one thing," he said.

Uh oh.

"It's a one bedroom apartment. We'd have to share a bed."

"Oh shit, then it's off," I said.

He pinched my dick.

"Ow! Okay you forced me into it," I said.

"There is one thing we need to talk about," he said.

"Our parents and friends," I said.

He nodded. "If we live in a one bedroom, they're going to figure it out that we're sleeping together. If they figure that out they'll figure out the rest. Are you cool with that?"

I put my head on his chest.

"I'd take a bullet for you. If our parents can't see that we love each other then it will be their loss. I think they'll come around eventually."

"I think so too. They'll shit at first but I think that they love us and want us to be happy."

I was as happy as a guy could be.

"Then I can't wait for us to become roommates," I said.

"Then we can do it every night," he said grinning.

"Let's do it now."

He rolled over on me and we made out for a long time. His boner was rubbing my butt crack and he began humping me. I raised my legs up and wrapped them around him and he was leaking enough that his dick slid in without any other lube. He fucked me gently and slowly and we kissed the whole time.

"I'm getting close," he said. "Do you want me to jack you?"

"No I have something in mind. Just fuck me and cum in me."

And he did just that. He pushed in deeply and I felt his cock throbbing inside me. After a while he slid out and we lay resting.

"What did you have in mind for your cock?" he said grinning.

"Jack me off… with your feet."

"What?"

"Brandon I have a little foot fetish thing. You have the most beautiful feet I've ever seen on a guy. I want you to put your feet on either side of my cock and jack me off."

"Kinky," he said. "I like it."

I lay back and he got to the end of the bed and lay on his back. He put his beautiful feet on either side of my cock and began to move them up and down it. Damn it felt amazing. I watched him, so beautiful working his feet over my cock and just marveled at how lucky I was.

Soon my cock began to tickle and I told him to speed up. He worked faster and suddenly I shot cum two feet into the air. A big gob landed on his feet and he kept milking it until I was dry. His feet were covered with cum.

I got up on my knees and leaned down and licked the cum off his gorgeous feet. Then I lay down on top of him.

"What did you think of that?" I said.

"That was pretty damn hot."

Suddenly we heard clapping. We looked up and across the gap between the houses and there was Teddy and Taco, both naked and sporting boners, watching us.

They were grinning like mad.

We had to laugh as Teddy lay on his back and Taco put his little brown feet on the sides of Teddy's cock and tried to do the same thing. Fucking little turds.

Brandon and I have now lived in the apartment for nearly 8 months. At first the parents didn't pay much attention but once they'd come to visit they saw that we both shared the one bed and the got the picture. Neither of us acts gay or dresses gay, so anyone who doesn't know our status has no idea we are lovers.

We both spend a lot of time studying and taking labs but we think it's worth it. When we both become doctors we can start a life together that will allow us to have pretty much anything we want.

I don't worry too much about it and neither does Brandon. We already have everything we want… each other.